## Jim Driver

was born in Yorkshire in 1954, and has spent most of his life successfully avoiding a 9-5 routine. He is a publisher, writes regularly for *Time Out* Magazine and has been working on his début novel for approximately twenty-three years. It is expected to appear soon (or shortly thereafter). He lives in south London with a large number of books, a television set and a stutter.

# *Rock* Talk

## edited by
## Jim Driver

The
**Do-Not**
Press

First Published in Great Britain in 1994 by
The Do-Not Press
PO Box 4215
London SE23 2QD

A Paperback Original

ISBN 1 899344 00 4

British Library Cataloguing in Publication Data. A catalogue record for
this book is available from the British Library.

Printed by The Guernsey Press Co Ltd, Channel Islands

# Contents

# Introduction

This is the first in a series of paperback originals centred around the best of today's new writing. 'Rock Talk' is concerned with rock 'n' roll, the next – 'Funny Talk' – will turn its beady eye on the world of comedy.

Many of the contributors to 'Rock Talk' have never had a word of prose published in their lives before. Musicians, broadcasters and promoters are rarely called on to put pen to paper, and when they are (I was repeatedly warned) the results can be pretty dire. Perhaps we were particularly lucky in finding such a rich seam of literacy, because the standard we found was so incredibly high. We'll (hopefully) be seeing more from many of these 'new' writers in the future. 'Rock Talk' also gave professional writers a chance to cover subjects *they* wanted to write about, rather than having to compromise and commercialise to please editors. All rose to the challenge, and many gave us their best work.

A few figures: just over two hundred people were asked to contribute to 'Rock Talk'. Forty-four replied. It soon became apparent that there was going to be a shortage of female contributors, and so the ratio of approaches to women was stepped up. But out of 144 approached, only a handful took the time to reply. Luckily the three who did make it into print make up for any imbalance, but I can't help thinking that if Pete Townsend can find the time to pen a note...

About the editing. Some people didn't want their copy edited at all, and (after a fight) it wasn't; others fought valiantly for individual words (and non-words) to stay in, and we gave in about 50% of the time. 'Rock Talk' isn't a literary text-book so, after some discussion, we decided to be as flexible as possible about style.

It's only rock 'n' roll, after all.

*– Jim Driver*

'At least it's not a CULTURAL desert!'

# The Contributors

• **RAY LOWRY** is widely known as *the* rock cartoonist and has had his work published in publications like the *Times, Punch, Private Eye* and the *NME*. • **GLEN COLSON** started as the office boy at Charisma Records, and has since worked as a record plugger, press officer, A&R man and general rock 'n' roll person. • **JOHN COOPER CLARKE** was the original (and best) punk-poet, who has since had his poems featured in the GCSE syllabus, co-starred with the Honey Monster in Sugar Puffs ads, and missed more deadlines than Bernard Matthews has had gobbles. • **NICK COLEMAN** is a highly respected rock journalist and writer. Julie Burchill recently listed him as one of the only four people capable of writing about music (she was another). • **WILKO JOHNSON** first found fame as the manic, ground-breaking guitarist with Dr Feelgood. According to *Q*, he was almost asked to join the Rolling Stones, but he continues to front his own band and tread an independent path. • **MARTIN ROACH** founded, owns and runs the Independent Music Press. The first book he wrote and published, 'The Eight Legged Atomic Dustbin', topped the bestseller lists, unexpectedly denying the spot to an expensive glossy book about the Rolling Stones. • **BRUCE IGLAUER** is the founder and owner of Alligator Records in Chicago, Illinois. His piece on Hound Dog Taylor is an up-dated version of the sleeve-notes to the 1982 'Genuine Houserocking Music' album. All four Hound Dog Taylor albums are available on Alligator. • **DAEVID ALLEN** was a founder member of both Soft Machine and Gong. The first volume of his near-autobiography has just been published. • **LAURA CONNELLY** is a British music journalist who now works as a freelancer in Los Angeles. • **JOHN B SPENCER** is a musician, songwriter and novelist. His latest 'cri/fi' novel, 'Quake City', will be published by The Do-Not Press in 1995. • **JON RONSON** won the Columnist Of The Year Award in 1993, he is the eponymous hero of BBC 2's 'The Ronson Mission', and is currently a columnist for *The Guardian* newspaper. His book, 'Clubbed Class' has just been published by Pavilion. • **MARY COSTELLO** is a regular broadcaster with London's BBC station, GLR. • **VINCE POWER** is the founder and owner of the Mean Fiddler Group. • **CHRIS JAGGER** is a successful writer and musician who has learned to live with the fact that potted biographies like this *always* mention that he's Mick Jagger's younger brother. • **MILES HUNT** is the former frontman of The Wonder Stuff, currently carving out a new career for himself as a presenter on MTV. • **DARREN BROWN** is better known as Wiz, lead singer and guitarist with Mega City 4. • **LAURA LEE DAVIES** is Music Editor of London's 'Time Out' Magazine. • **KEITH BAILEY** (aka Keith Missile Bass) is bassplayer with Here & Now and various versions of Gong. He is also a promoter and agent. • **RON KAVANA** is an experienced musician and writer who fronts his own band, and is an occasional aid worker. • **DOC COX** (aka **IVOR BIGGUN**) is a musician, humorist and broadcaster, who occasionally dresses up as a rooster and harasses people in Tesco's • **ROY HARPER** is an influential and very independent singer/songwriter with a massive loyal following. • **JOHN OTWAY** first found fame with his then partner, Wild Willy Barrett in the mid-'70s, but subsequent musical success eluded him, until the publication of his book, 'Cor Baby, That's Really Me!' in 1990, revived his fortunes.

# *Rock* Talk

# 1
# Glen Colson
## ...on Strat's Legacy.

### Tony Stratton Smith, 1933-1987

It was on a Van The Man tour in 1987 that my game of pool was interrupted by a phone call. It was my sister telling me that Tony Stratton Smith was dead. I missed a simple black over the pocket and lost £10.

Strat had a profound affect on all who came into contact with him. I first met him through my sister back in the mid-'60s, at one of Shel Talmy's parties in Knightsbridge. Dudley Moore was on piano and Twiggy was on Babycham. Strat was hyping The Creation into the charts by paying off the music press and begging his flatmate Jimmy Saville to play their new single 'Painter Man'. His other band, The Koobas from Liverpool, had just made one last desperate dive at the charts by recording 'Sally', complete with whistle solo in the middle eight. It would cost £600 to purchase both their debut LPs today.

Strat had a big reputation in sports journalism on Fleet Street, but he was keen to break into show biz. He was big buddies with Matt Busby and Pelé, and was ticketed on the ill fated Manchester United Munich air disaster flight. But a last minute change in plans meant he ended up reporting on the Welsh national side in a World Cup qualifier instead. He had covered two World Cups as a reporter and was responsible for the transfer of Jimmy Greaves from Chelsea to AC Milan.

When Brian Epstein died, Strat was approached as a possible replacement to manage The Beatles. Later he would befriend Prince Charles and help create The Princes Trust, become Chairman of The Sports Aid Foundation and a member of the Tote, but his first priority was always his beloved Charisma, the record label he launched after two years in the thick of the pop industry.

His rise was slow but sure, and in 1969 I started working for him. I would arrive at his office about ten in the morning and make myself useful delivering things and making coffee. By this time he had four bands: The Bonzo Dog, The Nice, Rare Bird and Van Der Graaf Generator. We all worked out of his one bedroom flat in Soho's Dean Street. He would rise about 11.30, head for the bathroom, ordering a coffee on the way, and field calls in the bath. Staff averted their gaze as they passed the phone through the door. The flat was small but it was home to about seven full time staff who managed, published, booked and mothered Strat's bands.

The Bonzos were breaking up at the time. Vivian Stanshall, sporting a freshly shaven head, announced the split at The Lyceum, explaining that they were 'going to give it the pill'. I was given leave of absence to drum with them on the remainder of the tour because regular drummer Legs Larry Smith only seemed to want to drink on stage

Back at the flat after the tour, it was decided that I should become the office publicist. Terry Slater (aka Terry The Pill) was coerced into taking me round the Soho pubs and introducing me to the likes of Keith Altham, Richard Green (the beast) and Dominic Beehan. Terry got his nickname because he is said to have sold Purple Hearts to The Beatles in Hamburg. Rumour has it that on one occasion when the club was raided, he jumped out of the window, dropped his pill bottle, and was arrested picking pills up from the gutter. Our local was De

Hems, the Dutch pub on Macclesfield Street. After a heavy drinking-session I would end up back at the flat, put to bed around three-thirty, much the worse for wear after three or four pints of lager.

My first press calls concerned The Nice who had just burned an American flag on stage at the Albert Hall during their version of Leonard Bernstein's 'America'. Funnily enough they were finding it difficult getting visas for their upcoming American tour.

In the weeks that followed, the office visited Ronnie Scott's *en masse* to see Genesis. Strat signed them on the spot, beating off stiff competition from Island and Threshold. He also signed Lindisfarne because he liked the harmonica on their demo tape, and Audience after they supported Led Zep at the Lyceum. Strat had begun to promote shows there under the name , The Midnight Court.

The office always tottered on the brink of disaster. It was a constant juggling act trying to keep all these bands on the road and recording. Once we had all gone without wages for two weeks, so Strat borrowed cash against his fees for editing *The International Football Yearbook*.

Charisma Records was launched with a Rare Bird single called 'Sympathy' which became a sizeable hit. Then The Nice released their 'Five Bridges Suite' on Charisma after their old record company, Immediate, had gone broke, owing them a small fortune. With the label up and running, plenty of hype was needed to keep the ship afloat. Strat would write fantastic three page letters to all and sundry, brimming over with the most preposterous claims.

After a typical day's work, the office would decamp to a private drinking club in Wardour Street called La Chasse. It was full of music biz types... roadies, Keith Moon, David Bowie, Stan Webb and all the office bands. After holding court at La Chasse, the Boss would head a procession down to The

Speakeasy, a night club just off Oxford Circus where you could eat and drink, watch Procol Harum or Jimi Hendrix play, meet The Beatles or argue with Ginger Baker.

It was an unwritten rule that if you had been in the front line all night you could turn up late for work the next day. Strat himself never rose much before lunchtime, unless the bank manager was on the phone or Keith Emerson was calling. Disaster struck when, after a gig in Luton, The Nice split up just as the world was about to land at their feet. Charisma released two more of their LPs, before Strat opted not to manage ELP in favour of the two outsiders in the band, an early sign of his sense of fair play.

The well-oiled Charisma machine went into top gear for Genesis, Van Der Graaf and Lindisfarne, who were packaged together and put out on the road for just sixty pence admission. Bigger tours were planned and Strat signed Monty Python and produced their first full length feature film. They went on to record six chart albums for Charisma.

Records, concerts, musicals, comedy, book publishing, politics, sport... Strat seemed to me to be involved in anything and everything. If he wasn't hanging out with Dennis Howell, he was down the Marquee drinking with agents, writers and bar staff. Fearful that he might forget something important in the haze of an evening, he would keep notes of the conversations, scribbling down ideas and suggestions on the back of a Silk Cut packet. His favoured drink was referred to as his poison – a large vodka and tonic. I don't ever recall him ordering a single vodka during in all the time I knew him. A peerless barroom philosopher, he never minded buying three rounds to your one.

The signing continued throughout the '70s: poet laureate John Betjeman, hip shrink RD Laing, and Viv Stanshall, who drank his way through two LPs and a film, 'Sir Henry At Rawlinson End'.

If Strat believed in you, he would go all the way. He had unnerving faith in all his acts and would brook no critique. He allowed me to produce LPs by John Arlott and Peter O'Sullivan, and work on his favourite project, a film entitled 'The Day A Team Died', the story of the Munich air disaster that wiped out half the Manchester United team in 1958. Travelling the world as a writer gave him a gold cover but it could be dangerous. Once he was stabbed in South America while on the hunt for Martin Bormann. He had already written 'The Rebel Nun', a biography of the martyr Mother Maria Skobtzov. There were times when he would mysteriously disappear for months on end... no-one close to him knew where he was or for whom he was working.

By the end of the '70s, Strat had tired of music and was becoming heavily involved in horse racing. He ploughed all his loot into buying horses and paintings. By now he had a flat in Regents Park and a house in the country, and Charisma was moving through a succession of offices. Somehow they were all within 200 yards of The Marquee, and Charisma eventually settled above the now gutted old site of the club in Wardour Street, where I would visit him with ideas and plans, hoping for the odd hand-out. Julian Lennon and Malcolm McLaren were late signings to Charisma, but by this time the label was only limping along, and it was only a matter of time before Strat accepted a bid of £4,000,000 from Richard Branson. He then retired to the Canaries as a tax exile and opened a night club called The Final Crease.

It was on a visit to Jersey that he fell ill and died in 1987. His ashes were scattered over Newbury Racecourse and that same afternoon his horse, Sergeant Smoke, romped home at 20-1. His great friend Jack Barrie, manager of The Marquee for 20 years, still runs a horse called Strat's Legacy. It races in Strat's old colours – red for Manchester United, green for Brazil and Purple for Charisma.

# 2
# John Cooper Clarke

## ...débuts a brand new poem.

### TOM JONES

Back in town in the black Rolls Royce
The funky hunky housewife's choice
In one thing he can rejoice
His trousers don't affect his voice.

# 3
# Nick Coleman

## ...on the sadness at the heart of music writing.

Many, many people write about music. Perhaps too many. Some of them write about music because they want to hang around with musicians. Some of them do it because they want to sleep with musicians. Others because they want to parade around on the catwalk of cultural discourse. But none of these people are to be trusted. Nor are they likely to be any good at writing about music. Not for long, anyway.

There are three qualifications necessary for writing about music. One is an interest in writing. Another is a fierce liking for music. The third is a particular kind of emotional scar tissue. You see, you can only be a good music writer if you have suffered horribly at a vulnerable stage in your life with the knowledge that, come what may, you are never going to be a musician yourself.

All the good music writers I know did. Not only did they endure the practical frustrations that arise from not being much good at music, but they also suffered neurotically, from the desperate, lingering realisation that they were not, ever, going to be the pop star of their choice.

For instance, one fine writer I know ached for some time with the knowledge that when he grew up he was not going to be Peter Wolf of the J Geils Band. Another, a son of Ipswich, felt the odds were stacked against him in his desire to be Stevie Wonder, so after some thought he decided to be Andy Partridge of XTC, having reasoned that, being English, white and provincial, he'd at least have some of the basics down. But no. He writes about music for a living. Life is pain.

As for myself, I was an arrogant fantasist, and was determined that I would keep my own name and identity while making entry like a knife into the general spirit, look and social demeanour of my favourite gang. I only settled to properly apostolic suffering, you see, when the Rolling Stones appointed Ron Wood as their official, salaried second guitarist. A black day. Because I'd spent every night for the best part of a year in the darkness of my bedroom, flat on my back on the bed, fitting myself in on imaginary strummed acoustic to the middle ground of 'It's Only Rock And Roll'. That's me going buh-dummm in the intro, you know. Nick 'n' Keith, The Rhythm Twins, we were called.

So you write about music instead. Writing does, after all, share certain characteristics with music. For a start, you can show off in writing. And writing can be sexy, for the writer if for no-one else (cf. Nicholson Baker). Also, there is rhythm in writing. And what are metaphors for if not to lend resonance and, in some cases, a quasi-harmonic structure to the drive of your sentences? Writing is every bit as good as music in all things, except in that it lacks the power to say things beyond the compass of verbal language.

So we do it, we unfulfilled ones, and hope against hope that in writing we strike chords, ring changes, develop themes, descant, and do all the things musicians do, while simultaneously doing something that musicians can't do, which is to locate music, bag it up, plant it in the fallow fields of language and context, where it can grow strange new blooms. Unsurprisingly, musicians often resent music writers for doing this.

To most musicians, music writers are a necessary evil, at best a useful device for pontooning a musician's music into the marketplace, at worst a sub-industrial caste of self-serving parasites. And, until recently, most musicians showed fierce resistance to the operations of writers. 'Don't put me in a box,' they'd snarl at the first hint of contextualising inquiry from a writer (I say 'recently' for the reason that changes in the contextual landscape of the music world have led to the appearance of a new kind of musician, whose interest is exercised primarily in the exploration of his or her context within the larger field of general culture: think of Madonna and Guns 'N Roses, for instance, both of whom exhibit more interest in the way they're mediated than in the way they 'play'). In general, musicians do not want to be poked and prodded, explored and explicated, made subject to the laws of verbal language. That's why they're musicians - to make the world a bearable, less strictured place for themselves to live in.

Unfortunately, music writers live for this kind of pokey exploration, and love to be subject to the strictures of verbal language. And there is a compulsion amongst good ones to get right inside, to inhabit, to explore music and its populous world, not because they want to belong there but because they want to carry off its belongings. They do it not for the benefit of musicians, nor on behalf of music's consumers, but for themselves. That's why they're music writers. We're not here to make the world a better place for everyone else but to make it a bearable one for ourselves.

Music writers have also always been very good at making themselves feel important. Both the good ones and the not-so-good ones. Some of the not-so-good ones, as I suggested before, do it by copping off with musicians, either imaginatively or literally. Others – those semi-detached Olympians who see where others only consume – do it by assuming magisterial status over musician and reader alike (there really are people who think that there are records you should buy, views you should hold and, most bizarrely of all, tastes you should *not* be victim to). While some regard themselves as nothing less than a continuation of the music world itself: as pop stars by proxy, responsible for the wordy embodiment of the values and ideas musicians are, well, too musicianly to take care of themselves.

Which is not to say that good music writers are not vulnerable to all of these temptations, and don't succumb from time to time to their allure. They do. But the good music writer, like the deep maverick he is in his dreams, ultimately derives a sense of his own importance from the abiding, and abidingly hurtful, conviction that he is not of the musical flesh: that he is neither friend nor enemy to musicians, nor an Olympian creature gifted with special powers of arbitration, nor a participant in any artistic or industrial endeavour save that of burglary to alleviate the poverty of his own soul. Most of all, he gets his importance from his unrivalled understanding of what it's like not to be a pop star.

I once had a very pleasant chat with a musician of formidable talent but not much real fame. He was interested in what it's like to write about music; to listen to music, to feel, think about and then formulate words around a property that to him had no need of words to make sense. He wanted to know if I really did need to *make* sense of music, implying that here was a perfect case of manufacture for the sake of it. He also wondered whether I wasn't simply making use of non-musical tools to counterfeit a musicianly feeling in myself. Then finally, and with a kind of sorrowful flourish, he accused me of wanting to trap music in words out of sheer blind jealousy, because I couldn't bear the thought that music might not be in me in the natural order of things. Like a fox-hunter, he said, who hunts the fox out of jealousy of its freedom.

He looked genuinely surprised when I went along with all of his assertions. He found it difficult to get to grips with the idea that people do things like that.

# 4
# Wilko Johnson

## ...remembers an evening spent with Mr Kardoom.

Mr. Kardoom was a massage-man who lived and worked on Bombay's waterfront, under the Gateway of India. Every evening I would go to where he sat, surrounded by his few possessions, take off my shoes and sit down on his little carpet. After a while he would ask me for two rupees and send a boy for some ganja.

He said that it was beneficial to the health to smoke ganja in the evening.

'But no *charas*. That makes you go mad.'

One evening when I arrived there were two or three other people there. They were talking excitedly and Mr Kardoom asked me for four rupees.

'Tonight we smoke *charas*. Bombay black.'

While we were waiting some more people joined us. One very lively guy had a plate of food which he pointed at emphatically – 'this is Indian eat! No eggs, no mutton!'

The boy returned with two small pellets of black hashish. Mr Kardoom mixed it with ganja and filled a chillum, which he lit and passed around. When it got to me I took two big hits. By the time I passed it on, I was extremely stoned. I had just begun to take stock of my surroundings when the chillum arrived at the food man. He took a blast which made him cough and a shower of sparks burst from the chillum. The character beside him slapped him on the shoulder and rolled over in convulsions of laughter. Soon we were all helpless, aching with mirth at the splendid display of sparks we had seen.

Eventually things quietened down and the others drifted off, until there was just me and Mr Kardoom.

Beyond the shoulder of the frayed blue blazer he always wore, I could see the waves lapping to the beach in the darkness. Huge reptiles were marching in infinite solemn processions from the sea up into the streets of Bombay.

I was in a temple staring at the wall where a thousand garish idols were expounding primeval truths with intricate mathematical gestures. They raised their arms and flowed into a massive brightly-coloured mandala.

In the centre sat Mr Kardoom. His eyes met mine.

'You walk in the sky?'

'Yes,' I said, and the word echoed and re-echoed in my skull. I stood up and took my leave and began the long walk up to the Victoria Terminus where I slept each night.

Some limousines had pulled up outside the Taj Mahal Hotel and a party of rich people were walking across the red carpet. The men were in immaculate evening dress and the women wore expensive glittering saris.

I suddenly realised how scruffy I was, and that I would soon be walking among them.

It was ludicrous beyond all bearing.

I stepped off the pavement and walked into the middle of the street, threw my head back and laughed out loud.

The Seventies were about to begin.

# 5

# Martin Roach

## ...'Gigaholic'

**1**00 Club for Jazz at 1pm, no charge. St. Martin-in-the-Fields at 3pm, Gorecki Symphony No.3, £9. Tube to Blues and Ballads Club in the Sols Arms, Flynn Brothers, 6.30pm, unknown charge. Borderline for Boltthrower and Headcleaner, 8pm, £5. Institute of Dubology at 11pm, Benjamin Zephaniah, £6. Cab to 606 Club for Andy Panayi Contemporary Jazz, Tenor sax, 12.30am, unknown charge.

I flipped my diary shut. Today's roster looked quite manageable. Almost pedestrian. Reasonable cost, probably no more than £30. Reasonable mix, but then I was never concerned for the sonic diet on offer, rather more that I should be there at all, listening, looking, consuming whatever was offered for digestion, palatable or not. I was concerned that I might not be able to make the last show of what was a relatively early night. The trip was only across one postal code but Brixton to Fulham was never an easy journey. Possible cancellation there. I hate cancellations. Nothing to do except hang around looking for another gig, which there weren't always around at such late notice, other than the most obscure of folk-crossover sets. I frequently found myself, when the vagaries of public transport or some pocket philosopher in a taxi had failed to deliver me on time, at the back of some smoke-sodden pub, halfway through a lock up, a probable conspiracy between the dreadful act and the publican. Serve the beer warm and the music tepid. Keep the beer flowing and the bastards listening.

First gig of the night. The 100 Club. One of my favourites. History. Poor bar but plenty of history. Not a bad band, even played some of their own stuff rather than harp on with bastardised Gillespie. He'd probably turn in his grave if he knew what was being played in his name. The next show at St. Martin-in-the-Fields had never taken lightly to my drinking and crinkly brown paper accompaniments to The Four Seasons. If only they knew it was just orange juice. Funny how they let the real drunks in with their own greasy brown bags but if you choose to tipple of your own volition you are frowned upon. Jesus' sweatbox dishing out its own perverted sense of judgement again. Still, Gorecki was a classic, and rarely performed. Surprisingly, the Church wasn't full. Unsurprisingly it was also the most expensive gig of the day. A Church gig. I laughed at the phrase. Perhaps the Nun at the door was a divine bouncer, and her habit was in fact a tuxedo for the righteous. Did that make God the promoter?

It was bad organisation on my part to hit the rush hour for the Flynn Brothers gig. I had seen them a few times before, about sixty, so I knew it would be worth my while, even though it was a lengthy tube journey. I was once told that if you travelled on the Northern Line twice a day for an average of twenty minutes for one year, you breathed in the equivalent of a human body full of hair and skin. If that was the case then I was worth a good first eleven. How many of those people who shared their body odours with each other daily ever considered their unwitting subterranean metastasis? I tried not to think of the four million people who used the tube everyday leaving either hair or skin or worse in the tunnels when they left for the surface, and the awful accumulative affect that such an enormous gathering would have. That was probably why they had so many delays on the tube - skin on the track, or a suspicious package of hair. 'When you leave the train, please be careful to take all your hair and skin with you.'

With the Flynn Brothers gig under my belt, I headed for the cafe in Frith Street where I usually filled my grumbling belly. Fill it up with some bread and fried rice, then on to the Borderline for the Boltthrower show. Good band, noise at its most violent, an aural mugging. The gig was full of groupies, sad little skirts with frail egos and enough insecurities to sink a battleship. I laughed at my own pompous conceit, sniggering at people's insecurities. Laughable. So young. One in particular reminded me of a girl at school. Apparently everyone had 'had' her. I didn't know what it meant but if anybody asked I said I had as well. All I knew was that she would show her front bottom to anyone for the price of a Sherbet Dip and a Wagon Wheel. But that was in old money.

I lifted myself up from the table, brushed the bread-crumbs that had trapped themselves in the depths of my brown cords and headed for the next show. Benjamin Zephaniah. Only seen him 12 times before so relatively he was a complete new-comer. The Institute of Dubology was an intimidating place, but by now my mind was plunging into its habitual maelstrom of torturous self-analysis and pathetic examination. Gradually my circle of friends, which had never been very large anyway, had dwindled away, confused by my odd habit, annoyed by my unreliability and the seemingly pointless pursuit of my compulsion, my need to see these gigs, these concerts. Even once I had the bit of paper that said I was officially abnormal and outside of the accepted realms of acceptability, they still frowned, even more so in fact because now they had official backing for what they had been whispering for years them-selves. It was as if the diagnosis was a confirmation of their doubts, their misunderstandings, when in fact it was a confirmation of only one thing and that was my complete and utter inability to stay away. The doctors had been perplexed, bewildered, but I didn't see what the problem was. I went to the gigs, I kept myself to myself, I didn't drink or drug to excess, never bothered anybody. I just stood at the back, listening, looking, watching.

They couldn't see that although I was not part of the crowd and I hated myself for that, this was the only way I felt I could get near, get close to that life. It was no good pretending I was anything other than an outsider, I had stopped that a long time ago. But this was my way of feeling adequate, important. That's why I enjoy even the gigs that are mostly empty, because then I can reconcile myself in the knowledge that I am part of some secret society in the know about that act, no matter how bad. The year had started off well, with over 350 gigs in the first four months. This was my 1,023rd gig that year, and Christmas was still eight days away. Not bad. Not that I had much choice.

Cab to 606 Club for Andy Panayi Contemporary Jazz Tenor Sax. 12.30. Unknown charge. Last gig of the night. Strange as it was, I was now coming to like the lifestyle, and as my attendances continued the people I saw almost became my work colleagues, my associates. I had become embroiled more and more in the completely anonymous circle of the replacement friends I had created at these concerts. None of them knew of me or cared for me, and I didn't mind.

All I needed was that they be there, standing in the same place as usual, drinking the same beer, so that I felt I knew them in some small way. The actual music had long since ceased being essential, and I usually managed to listen to even the worst offerings. When my condition worsened and my friends finally disowned me, my compulsion was exacerbated by that loneliness, which in turn propelled me to more gigs and so on until I was locked in a spiralling ride of isolated musical saturation. The irony was that I was only at my happiest when at a gig, yet this was the very same thing that had fuelled my sadness. Still, as Panayi's set drew to a close, I felt the same warm feeling of achievement that spread through my belly at the end of each night's journey. I had completed another day. I looked at my watch. Tomorrow was already here. Another day, another schedule. Best get some sleep. I might go to a gig tomorrow.

'That's why they call it the blues...'

# 6
# Jim Driver

## ...delves deep in to an addled mind to recall incidents from the early years of a would-be hippy entrepreneur.

The Driver family moved from Yorkshire to south west Wales on the very day Radio One began broadcasting. It was September 2nd, 1967.

Woken at some ungodly hour by torrential Welsh rain, thirteen-year old James Driver opened his bleary eyes and switched on the grime-encrusted transistor radio at his bedside. A youthful Tony Blackburn (ably assisted by a pre-recorded dog called Arnold) gushed forth in a totally sincere manner, before spinning a disc called 'Flowers In The Rain' by The Move. It was immediately after the celebrated Summer Of Love ('flower power', etc), his family had just moved house, and – in Tenby at least – the rain was pouring down. Had young James been a more clued-in kind of dude, he would have spotted some significance in all of this. As it was, he didn't even think it odd that everybody at Fabulous Radio One wore a tie.

James became Jim within four minutes of setting foot in the Greenhill School playground, and at precisely the same moment, his sister found herself transformed from a Gillian to a Gill.

Jim's chronic stutter didn't exactly help him pass unnoticed through the rough and tumble of school life. He'd often lie awake at night, and – once he'd wiped himself – would reflect on why he always seemed short of pocket money. Whenever he ordered a '99' from the whisky-breathed ice cream man in the school playground, he would invariably end up with nine choc-ices and little change. Yessir, when you're driving the verbal equivalent of a Reliant Robin, life in the fast lane can be pretty hazardous.

On the positive side, Jim's stammer did make him privy to some special insights: he could state with some certainty that telepathy doesn't exist – at least not in the people who tried to finish his sentences for him. And later he would discover that every taxi driver has a brother who *used* to stutter 'worse than wot you do, guv.' Inevitably he would have been cured by a process that takes several hours to describe, and climaxes in his joining the SAS or getting sent down for armed robbery.

Stammer or not, somehow Jim made it into the sixth form, and in his final year was appointed prefect. A brief battle raged inside his conscience between the two extremists who lived there: the monster of power-mania versus the sharing, caring would-be hippy. Needless to say, power mania won by a knock-out in the first round, and Jim spent the rest of the school year shopping other kids for minor breaches of discipline. Eventually, and against every prediction of the academic tipsters, he bagged himself a brace of mediocre A-levels, and his route to further education was assured. The world (in the words of his dyslexic careers master) was his ostery.

Jim's friends at the time had names like Loony and Pansy, and this – combined with a new-found reluctance to get his hair cut – gave his father some cause for concern. His friends would come and see him at his Saturday job at Woolworth's, and, after being thrown out by the manager, would hang around in the market square, before accompany-

ing him on underage drinking binges at the nearby Hope &
Anchor. Jim's preferred tipple in those days was a rather
cheeky little keg beer called Worthington E, a distant cousin of
the famed Watney's Red Barrel.

On the day he left school for good, Alice Cooper's
'School's Out' was leaping up the charts, but the feeling of
euphoria was seriously dampened when he heard that Donny
Osmond's 'Puppy Love' was still hugging the number one
position after four long weeks. The landlords of the Hope &
Anchor received a sizeable boost to their holiday fund that
night, although a gang of builders in the public bar vowed to
castrate Alice Cooper should he ever be foolish enough to set
foot in Tenby.

His friends had applied to study at bastions of education like Bristol University, The University Of Wales, and
Lampeter Theological College, but Jim bucked against the
trend and plumped for Mid-Essex Technical College in
Chelmsford. He had absolutely no plans to become a lawyer,
but he had noticed that there was a glut of law degree places on
offer. It seemed like a good idea at the time, but Jim's first lec-
ture (on Constitutional Law, as luck would have it) was enough
to convince him otherwise.

Dazzled by the bright lights of Chelmsford (usually
running at 20 watts), Jim spent his entire term's grant – a rather
handsome £135 – in the first two weeks. But to be fair, he did
have a lovely pair of blue suede boots and an absolutely fabulous ex-RAF overcoat to show for it, even if the assistant manager at Barclay's Bank (Melbourne Road) didn't approve of
either frippery. But the Man-in-the-Burton's suit did eventually
grant Jim a £40 overdraft to see him through the rest of the
term. It lasted three more weeks.

As all parents fear, even before Ian Dury put it to music,
college life has a nasty habit of revolving around Sex, Drugs

and Rock 'n' Roll – if not necessarily in that order. Jim's first priority were the drugs. Although he had never so much as taken a toke on a Number 6 (*fashion note:* a Player's 'Number 6' was a tiny and primitive form of cigarette, quite popular in the '70s, and very easy to lose in a matchbox), Jim had already worked out that the key to getting seriously involved in the counter culture was by getting as many drugs as possible in to his bloodstream.

There was only one problem. Not only did Jim not have the faintest idea how one did this, he didn't even know what they looked like, let alone what they *did*. One particularly cringe-worthy incident came about when he invited people to smell his Old Spice-tainted ex-RAF greatcoat. He had, he told them, dropped some hash on it.

Just days after arriving in Chelmsford, Jim attended the METC Fresher's Ball. It was one of those particularly exciting college affairs that abounded back in the '70s, and it starred two of the least promising bands on the London pub circuit. But the Worthington E flowed like water, so Jim was as happy as a pig in apple sauce.

Quite late in the evening, he was having a leak in the gents' changing room at the gym – as the concert hall was called the other 165 hours of the week – when a stranger shuffled up and whispered in his ear. The man had long dark-brown hair, parted down the middle, a long dark-brown beard that wasn't, and he wore pink-tinted granny glasses and a knee-length dark-brown fur coat.

'Pssst. Want to score some dope?' Hissed the long dark-brown beard.

'How much?' Asked Jim out of the corner of his mouth. He could scarcely believe his luck.

'How about a 50p deal?' replied The Beard.

'Okay.'

The transaction was completed, and Jim even managed to beg some Rizlas and matches off The Beard, who confided that his name was John. Jim later discovered that he was generally known around town as Hippy John. Jim spent the rest of the evening in a toilet cubicle, trying to get the chunk of cannabis, which he'd rolled inside a single cigarette paper, to light and stay lit – preferably without falling out. Jim didn't get very stoned that night.

Jim shared 'digs' with two other law students in the home of a man we shall call Alec. Alec, it transpired, had originally wanted three female students to share his council house, and had been very upset to find Jim, Steve and Alan foisted upon him. Alec was the sort of guy you see stalking through the supermarket with the basket under his arm crammed with a single type (and flavour) of instant crunchy dessert. He was the dodgy side of forty, divorced, wore thick pebble glasses and was as thin as a malnourished rake. In short, Alec not only was a 'bit of a case', he looked the part as well.

Jim's room-mate, clued-in Steve from East Ham, knew how to roll proper joints. He took Jim's 50p deal and transformed a sliver of it into something readily consumable. So, under Steve's expert guidance, he took his first deep drag of marijuana – and of tobacco. Jim felt a little strange. Jim felt like he was floating. Jim felt even stranger. Jim was sick. But he savoured the moment: it had been a revelation. He now knew everything there was to know about drugs.

Sex was an animal of a different kind. Despite several near-misses, at the age of eighteen Jim was still a virgin. But he was determined not to be one at nineteen, or even at eighteen-and-a-half. His first major attempt at getting his 'end away' in Chelmsford turned out to be a disaster. How many prospective former-virgins have made the mistake of targeting the least attractive person in the room, on the grounds that they will (quite naturally, you'd think) be so glad of the attention, they'll rip your clothes off you before you can say 'Eat A Peach'? Experience proves that this never, ever, works.

At the first Law Faculty disco of term, Jim targeted a stout young woman with a complexion you could have grated carrots on. Several sloppy kisses, two badly grazed cheeks, and a punch in the mouth later, he realised that he didn't want to shag her quite enough to get engaged – even if her brother was reputed to work at the Abbey Road recording studios, *and* was supposed to be a personal friend of George Harrison.

An early realisation that this kind of sexist tactic doesn't work led Jim – in a drunken stupor at an otherwise long forgotten party – to aim his affections at the best-looking woman in the place. After he had stuttered his way through asking her to dance (the usual 37 syllables), she pretended to faint. For the rest of the evening Jim channelled his affections towards a more amenable can of Watney's Party Seven. As the dawn loomed, it too feigned unconsciousness.

The rock 'n' roll aspect to Jim's life proved more fruitful. The Students' Union at METC in those days consisted of a pair of Portacabins® housing a part-time secretary called Cathy, an ageing professional student called Leo, and a duplicating machine of unknown identity. This machine produced the college magazine, which was expertly edited by a beer-swilling, scarf-wearing Scot called Ian MacDonald. At a chance meeting in the Railway Tavern, he let slip that he needed an assistant.

Enter a stuttering first-year student, whose offer of help was somehow misconstrued into an invitation to write half the magazine and staple it together every fortnight. But it did bring the eager, young, would-be hippy into contact with the world of rock 'n' roll. He was given a column to write, and put in charge of the music and books sections. This involved reviewing records (if any actually arrived), books (ditto), gigs, and – best of all – interviewing visiting rock stars.

Chelmsford boasted a council-run venue called the Chancellor Hall, and on Sunday nights a guy called Barry Somethingorother used to put on second division rock bands. For some reason he used to let Jim in free to review them, and allowed him to conduct lengthy celebrity interviews in the dressing-room afterwards.

But the interviews didn't always work out as planned. In fact they seldom did. One of the less successful dressing-room exchanges might go something like this:

JIM: 'Hey, that was a g-g-great show, M-m-m-m-m-m-m-man.'

STAR: '(smirking) Do you really think so?'

JIM: 'Of course. Absolute d-d-d-dynamite.'

STAR: '(smirking fit to burst) Er, thanks. But can we get on with the interview now? We've got some chicks to see after the gig, and we don't have a lot of time.'

JIM: ' Okay. Have you guys been on the r-r-r-r-r-road, long?'

STAR: '(laughing) Have we been on the what long?'

JIM: 'The R-r-r-r-r-r-r -r… the r-r-r-r-r-r-r-r-r-r-r-r… the r-r-r-r-r-r-r-r-r-r-r-r… Oh, sod it.'

SUBSEQUENT REVIEW: *'This reviewer has been to some terrible gigs in his time and has witnessed some crap performances, but this was undoubtedly the most inept he has ever witnessed. You can understand that sometimes things don't work out on certain nights, but the — Band proved themselves to be complete musical assholes, barely capable of playing two consecutive notes in tune and …'*

Ah, the power of the press.

What some students didn't like about the gigs at college was that they were run by a syndicate of past and present students. The social secretary at the time was called Steve, who had by then left college and was working at the Stock Exchange. One of his partners was called John Fogarty, an ambitious and very sharp east Londoner who was studying to be a company secretary. The other partner was Leo. They called themselves MESS and among their other activities, they owned the amusement machines in the students' lounge.

By this time, Jim had been slung out of Alec's council house for not being a girl, and he had found himself billeted with a group of final-year law students in a semi-detached house in the nearby village of Writtle. Writtle had long ceased being a village in the accepted sense of the word, and – despite its picturesque duck pond and ivy-clad pubs – was little more than an up-market barracks for commuting stockbrokers and bankers. Jim's house-mates turned out to be a pretty influential bunch. Their names were Helen, Joan and Mick. Mick (despite his Socialist Worker's Party membership card) was the undoubted leader of the pack, and he had one near-fatal flaw. When he was drunk, he would talk out of the side of his mouth. If you happened to point it out to him, he would get very stroppy indeed. A typical night in the pub would invariably end up with him talking out of the side of his mouth, Jim being pissed enough to mention it, and the two of them arguing until the wee small hours.

Jim's involvement with the magazine kept him in touch with happenings at the Students' Union. Methodist youth leader Leo had become union president and was very much in charge at the twin Portacabins®. He was taking a degree in business studies or something equally specious, and spent his spare time thinking up ways of altering the Union constitution so as to keep himself in a sabbatical post until retirement. Jim was asked by a group of people (one of whom was speaking to him out of the side of his mouth at the time) to stand in the forthcoming Students' Union elections as social secretary.

The chances of a first year student, barely a month into his course, getting elected as social secretary were rated as none minus ten. But Jim stood unopposed, and despite a high turn-out and a strong 'no' vote, he got the job. Up to that point he had attended lectures fairly regularly, but following his election, Jim made an unconscious decision to give law the elbow. After all, it was bloody hard work, and it needed someone with a memory equal to a that of a hundred particular clever elephants. And anyway, Jim wasn't cut out for a legal career: it was time-consuming enough just being a full-time rock 'n' roller.

In these post-Thatcherite days, it's very difficult to imagine the mood of those times. The air was thick with the twin whiffs of incense and bullshit, and a new dawn was confidently expected any day. Censorship was being done away with and the youth (who in those days were the idealists) were working towards getting things changed. How were they to know that within two decades, it'd be their counterparts who'd be the ones demanding more government crackdowns and less hand-outs to scroungers?

In 1972, it was all very well pretending to be radical, but in retrospect, there wasn't anything to get particularly radical about. In those days there were still plenty of mines turning out plenty of coal, the National Health Service was still free and functioning, the railways ran more trains, more often, and usually on time. The idea of 17.5% VAT (VAT was 8% then) on fish and chips and household fuel was an outlandish nightmare, best left to one of the more outrageous Douglas Adams novels.

Jim and the rest of his pseudo-hippies were part of an *alternative* alternative society. Part of their job involved going to parties and being slung out by the 'straights' for sitting on the floor. Part of it involved being able to laugh about it afterwards and feel good about not having to go to work the morning after. But most of all, it involved believing that nothing really mattered. Despite still being a virgin and a dope-smoker of just a few weeks, Jim had managed to convince most people (including himself) of his impeccable alternative credentials.

He even got himself a groupie.

One lunchtime Jim was sitting in the Railway Tavern, eating his pair of cheese and tomato rolls (he was a greedy bastard even then) and sipping a frosted glass of lemonade and lime, when in walked a young, lanky girl with straight black hair and purple loons. She spoke to Les at the bar for a second, nodded, and then plonked herself down next to the guzzling Jim.

'You book all the music for the college, don't you?' she asked.

'Y-y-y-y-yes,' conceded Jim between munches.

'I want to help you,' said Mary. 'I want to be your assistant. Okay?'

Jim nodded and swallowed the blob of damp cheese, tomato and once-crusty roll that lay at the back of his mouth.

Mary turned out to be just fifteen years old. 'Jailbait' as Jim's friends kept warning him. But it didn't matter. Although she was quite amenable to any form of sexual molestation and would just lay there and stare at the ceiling if any were attempted, it turned out that Mary had a problem. For reasons best left to the *Gynaecologist's Weekly*, she couldn't er, ...do it.

So Jim turned his sexual attentions to a woman he'd met at a party. Her name was Sandra. It seemed to Jim that she knew everybody and that everyone knew her. They did, most of them in the biblical sense. Sandra was, she was proud to relate, a leading member of the Galleywood players, an amateur theatrical group of some note. But her best act was to pretend not to be available for sex. It fooled no-one but Jim.

Jim was slightly more successful as social secretary. He had been going down to London to investigate the *real* alternative society and had stumbled upon the Sunday night gigs at the Roundhouse. Based around a theme of debauchery, drugtaking and four or five bands a night, they went under names like The Greasy Trucker's Ball and The Wonder Wart Hog's Second Ball.

What usually happened at these events was that a few reasonably well-known 'alternative' bands like Hawkwind, Man and The Groundhogs would rotate with lesser known acts such as Magic Michael and Om, with a DJ filling the gaps with indeterminable Quintessence and Grateful Dead album tracks. A thousand or more people would pay good bread (as money was called in non-bakery circles in those days) to get in, and sit cross-legged on the floor, smoking dope and chomping on watery-but-hard brown rice and bland lentil stew. And very nice it was, too.

Jim's idea was to recreate all this, on a much reduced budget, for the good buggers of Chelmsford. His first attempt at alternative promotion was – ironically, perhaps – a tremendous commercial success. He booked The Third Ear Band, a tedious but strangely hip avant-garde troupe who had just won plaudits for their soundtrack to Polanski's film 'Macbeth'; a local trad jazz band who were acquainted with magazine editor Ian MacDonald; a Welsh rock outfit of dubious musical ability; and a really hip hippy lightshow from Shepherds Bush. The Mach II Disco from Writtle were roped in, under strict orders to ditch their usual Sweet and Chicory Tip collection in favour of things they didn't actually like. The gig, dreary as it was, sold every ticket the SU could lay their collective hands on. And, best of all, it was so 'alternative' no one dared moan about the boring bits (*ie* the part between the doors opening and the end). Jim really did believe he had created something worthwhile. Life was like that back in 1972.

Jim was incredibly glad he had been introduced to a large gentleman called Harry. Harry was the man who organised security – for 'security' read 'bouncers' – for the gigs at METC. At the end of the night, after Jim had given Harry £36 for the six stewards he had provided, Harry gave him back a crisp £5 note. That was apparently the way it worked, it was the same all over the world, and who was new-born hippy Jim to argue with the status quo? After all, he needed it: he had an overdraft of £51.36.

The following Monday morning, Jim was treated like a king in the SU offices. He had made a profit of nearly £60 on his first gig. It was the first profit METC SU had made on a gig in living memory and (he was told) it could mean the end of the entertainment subsidy – for ever. A slight shiver went down his spine, but Jim couldn't work out why. Perhaps somebody had walked over his grave. Yes, he was that naive.

But Jim didn't have time to think about mundane matters like money. SU President Leo was breaking the habit of a lifetime by authorising the use of SU petty cash for buying plastic cups of coffee from the machine. Cathy was even sent out to get some imitation-cream cakes, which were duly cut in half and shared round. They certainly knew how to celebrate in those days.

Jim's honeymoon period was soon to fizzle to an end. Everybody on the Students' Union executive, apart from him and one other guy, were what were known as 'straights'. The exception was the Internal Vice President, a guy called Pete, who later got slung out of his course, and who would eventually join HM Customs & Excise as a drug investigator. Everybody thought that this was a particularly suitable career for Pete, as he would have no problem in identifying any drug that was put before him. He didn't turn up for many SU meetings and was soon replaced as IVP by the smooth-talking, sharp-dressing, John Fogarty.

One day part-time secretary Cathy tried to warn Jim that Leo didn't like him and would try and get rid of him. She made sure they were alone and glanced carefully around, before pulling off her thick horn-rim glasses and whispering in his ear: 'Jim, I think you should watch out for Leo, he's...'

Jim watched open-mouthed as she gasped, jumped three feet in the air, replaced her glasses and resumed typing a report for Leo on the advantages of having a full-time union president.

'What do you mean, Cathy?' Jim began, then turned round to discover the diminutive, cropped-haired figure of Leo, standing menacingly behind him. It was just like that bit in 'The Ipcress File' when Michael Caine...

'Hello, Jim,' smiled Leo without a trace of humour in his voice. It was, thought Jim, exactly like that episode in 'Marathon Man' where nasty Laurence Olivier creeps up behind nice Dustin Hoffman (with their sizes reversed) and...

The gigs came and went, and continued to make money. Jim spent most of his time avoiding his lecturers (he was still naive enough to think that they gave a damn what he did with his life), drinking Gray's bitter in the Railway Tavern, and meeting up with his new friend Hippy John in order to consume marijuana and takeaway Chinese curries. Most of Jim's money at the time came from small scale kick-backs from the college gigs, including a very amenable arrangement he had worked out with a local PA company.

He was persuaded by a group of 'concerned students' led by Mick (he of the sideways conversations) to do a benefit for the drug-help charity Release. The Students Union (ie Leo) were worried about the possible ramifications of dabbling in drugs (metaphorically speaking), but Jim found unexpected support from John Fogarty, and together they beat the rest of the executive into submission. Ageing Young Methodist Leo had to go away and bang his tambourine a few times, but eventually even he came to like the idea.

A line-up came together that included The Edgar Broughton Band, Nazareth, The Global Village Trucking Company and Radio One DJ Alan Black. Edgar Broughton was the doyen of the alternative culture at the time and they had just finished a nationwide seaside tour, playing to alarmed holiday-makers from the back of a truck. Nazareth were a rock band on the way up, and the Global Village TC, who were a rich man's commune band, featuring the children of various aristocrats. They including a sallow youth called Jeremy Lascalles who was destined to become a leading record company executive.

One fly in the ointment was the abdication of Nazareth to play a gig at the Rainbow, but The Sensational Alex Harvey Band galliantly stood in. Posters were designed by a tall, straight-black-haired, unsmiling female art student called Jenny. Jenny could have found work as a stereotypical art student extra in one of those stereotypical dramas they had on BBC2 at the time, had it not been for the fact that she loved her art too much. The posters were printed by 'friends' at the *Daily Mirror* for little more than the cost of the (news)paper.

Leo had a near-coronary when one band (no names mentioned, eh, Rob?) demanded half their expenses money in the form of cannabis resin, and certain other people were quite upset that uniformed security guards with dogs were employed to control the crowds. The attendance exceeded the fire limit by some 250%, and even then there were five hundred people stuck outside, all claiming to have come from Glasgow and all saying that they'd lost their tickets. The benefit raised £750 for Release (nearly two year's grant for Jim) and he got his picture in the local papers and in the infamous *Oz*.

About a week after the Release Benefit, Jim was in the main Chelmsford post office, buying a stamp for one of his routine begging letters to his parents. Behind him a small, bearded man with longish black hair was arguing with a fragile-looking hippy girl about some money they couldn't get their hands on. He looked like a miniature John Peel with hair, and she was the spitting image of the girl on the 'Woodstock' posters. Inevitably, they got talking.

The diminutive Peel was, as he told Jim, by sheer coincidence a Radio North Sea pirate DJ called Roger West, and the woman was his girlfriend, Lee. Their car had broken down on the way from Clacton, and they were waiting for some money to be wired to them from the radio station's offices in Holland. All the facts fitted: the pirate radio ship, the Mi Amigo *was* moored off Clacton, and Jim seemed to recognise the name Roger West from the many blurred late night hours he and his cronies had spent listening to the crackly progressive rock station. And when pressed, Roger could do a very passable Album Chart Countdown, complete with jingles, time checks and suitable sound-effects.

Good enough.

Have no fear, Jim told Roger and Lee, he would look after them until their money arrived. And, as coincidence would have it, he was on his way round to see some people at a very suitable 'crash pad' in Broomfield Road. The house was a very suitable place for near-penniless pirate radio DJs and their girlfriends to stay while waiting for funds to arrive from The Hague. It was owned by the rich Indo China-based parents of a girl called Natalie, and she didn't seem to mind who stayed there. Which was probably just as well, as it turned out.

It soon became apparent that top radio DJ Roger West was hooked on barbiturates, or 'reddies', as he called them. The name came because his favoured brand came in capsules that were almost as bright a red as his eyes. Lee wasn't quite so keen on popping pills, but she didn't seem to mind Roger talking non-stop for an hour or two in a progressively greater slur, before finally keeling over and falling asleep at her feet. She didn't even mind him doing the Album Chart Countdown (complete with jingles, time checks and sound-effects) sixteen times a night, either.

But to give Roger credit, he didn't mind sharing out his little red capsules. From his first night in town, there would inevitably be five or six people – including Jim and Roger – passed out at Lee's feet every night around 2am. If she did mind, she didn't say anything. Natalie didn't even mind that a wardrobe that had stood in the corner of the front room for several years was reduced to matchwood within an hour of Roger's arrival, as successive bodies – helped along by the 'reddies'– repeatedly crashed into it on their way to the toilet.

But for all his charm and generosity, by his second week in Chelmsford, it had become obvious that if Roger West were indeed Roger West, then he was certainly not employed as a DJ on Radio North Sea. He kept up the pretence to the end, and even had a good percentage of Chelmsfordians convinced – Jim included – that there really was a dial on the Mi Amigo that registered the number of listeners tuned-in, by the power-drain on the ship's transmitter.

Jim stood outside many a phone box, dutifully listening as Roger 'called up' the radio station's offices in Holland and told them off in no uncertain terms for sending the money to the 'wrong Chelmsford' or for 'forgetting to fill in the right code word'. Jim knew that Roger was only pretending to dial the number, and that his finger would stay on the receiver-bar throughout the call. But he never told a soul: after all, he was the one who had introduced Mr West to Chelmsford in the first place.

Despite his many attempts at luring Lee in to bed the very second Roger's eyelids closed each night, Jim was failing miserably on all sexual fronts and was still a virgin. But with a famous pirate DJ in the house, every night at Broomfield Road was party night, and a never-ending string of bright young things passed through the building, ever-eager to appear sophisticated and hip.

On the third night of Roger and Lee's stay, the circus included a voluptuous young student called Sue, who was almost as beautiful as she was big. With their minds deliciously dulled by a well-judged excess of drink and drugs, Jim and Sue began to kiss and fondle. After a good hour's encouragement from Sue, he finally whipped off her jeans, and inserted his thingy into her wotsit. Then he noticed that Lee was looking right at him as he and Sue writhed together behind a tall pile of Afghan coats on the floor. Horrified, he quickly pulled himself off, and desperately thought of some excuse to stop. He, er... could pretend to have found religion... er, needed to go to the toilet... er, had cramp... er, or something. It never occurred to him to check that Lee was even awake. She was in actual fact, fast asleep. Never did it once cross Jim's mind that Lee wouldn't have cared either way what he did. But Jim still had high hopes in that department.

Technically, he was no longer a virgin, but after a long deliberation, Jim's decision was that he still hadn't 'done it' properly.

And for some reason he couldn't fathom, Sue didn't want to have anything to do with such a creature after that night. She gave him an icy stare and a kick in the bollocks every time he got so far out of it as to suggest they finish off what they'd started.

Jim never quite admitted it – even to himself – but he quite liked the way Sue did that.

### Epilogue

*Roger West and Lee disappeared one day without a word. Jim eventually found sexual fulfilment with a Polish princess called Yana, before being kicked out of college for leading a student sit-in, and/or for not attending lectures.*

*Jim went off to write babble for a couple of long-dead underground newspapers, before finding paid work as a bus conductor in Chelmsford, and unpaid work as an office boy for a very small, but very hippy record company in Shepherd's Bush.*

*Which takes us up to the autumn of 1973...*

# 7

# Bruce Iglauer

## ...remembers Hound Dog Taylor and The HouseRockers.

They ran on equal parts of brotherly love, vicious adolescent rivalry and Canadian Club. For over ten years Hound Dog Taylor and the HouseRockers made joyous music together five or six nights a week, first in the tiny taverns that dot Chicago's South Side ghetto, later in clubs colleges and concert halls literally around the world.

They were quite a sight on the bandstand. Hound Dog perched on his folding chair, stomping both feet to keep time, grinning his millions-of-teeth grin, pausing between songs only long enough to light up a Pall Mall and tell a totally incomprehensible joke (which he'd interrupt halfway through, cackling with laughter and burying his face in his hand) before tearing into another no holds-barred boogie. Phillips (no one ever called him Brewer) with his broken teeth and crooked smile, dancing in the aisles, his vintage Fender Telecaster strung around his neck like some giant pendant, his shirt tail hanging out, kicking his leg in the air as he squeezed out a high note, occasionally grabbing the mike to sing in a voice as battered as his guitar. Ted Harvey, his hair clipped tight to his head, yelling out encouragement from behind his minimal drum set, chomping out the rhythm on the wad of gum in his mouth, sometimes drifting off to sleep without ever missing a beat, until Phillips would sneak up behind him in mid-song and wake him with a slap across the back of the head.

They were inseparable, and they played together like brothers, sensing each other's musical twists and turns before they happened, feeding energy and good spirits from one to the other. They fought like brothers, too, as they criss-crossed the country from gig to gig in Hound Dog's old Ford station wagon, arguing constantly about who was the best lover, who had the best woman, who was the best mayor Chicago ever had, who was or wasn't out of tune the night before. The arguments weren't always in fun either From time to time a knife appeared, and finally even a gun.

They made a lot of noise for three men with two guitars and a drum set. Between the incredible distortion from Hound Dog's super-cheap Japanese guitar, the sustain from his brass-lined steel slide (made from the leg of a kitchen chair), the sheet metal tone of Phillips' ancient Fender, their cracked-speaker amplifiers, and Ted's simple, kickass drumming, they could indeed rock the house.

They played amazingly long sets, two or three hours of driving boogies and shuffles mixed with the occasional slow blues. It was music born in the Deep South juke joints, when electric guitars were still something new and bass guitars were unheard of, music for all-night dancing and partying. The purists called them a blues band, but Hound Dog called it rock and roll.

Hound Dog was already playing guitar and piano when he came to Chicago from Mississippi in 1942 at the age of 27. (He used to haul an upright piano to Delta fish fries on a mule drawn wagon). But he was strictly an amateur musician. He moved in with his sister Lucy in the neighbourhood around 39th and Indiana in the heart of the ghetto, a neighbourhood he lived in for the rest of his life. He found a day job as a short order cook, and on Sunday mornings he played for tips at the

Maxwell Street open-air market, competing for attention with unknowns like Muddy Waters and Robert Nighthawk.

It wasn't until 1975, when Hound Dog lost his last job building TV cabinets, that he began trying to make his living as a musician. He played with almost every guitarist and drummer in the city until he chose a construction worker named Phillips in 1959 and a shipping clerk named Ted in 1965 as the official HouseRockers.

By pricing his band lower than any other on the South Side (when I met them in 1970, the whole band was making $45 a night), Hound Dog was able to get gigs at taverns that usually couldn't afford a band. And by pumping out non-stop music and clowning, he drew one of the most loyal crowds in town. Hound Dog and the HouseRockers played some of the seediest clubs in Chicago, clubs that held fifty or a hundred people (who were usually dancing frantically in the aisles), clubs that didn't even have a bandstand, just a space cleared of tables where the band could squeeze in. Their favourite gig was the Sunday afternoon jam at Florence's at 54th Place and Shields, a gig they held for over ten years. On Sundays at Florence's, you were likely to run into Big Walter Horton, Magic Slim, Carey Bell, Lefty Dizz, Son Seals, Lee Jackson, Big Moose Walker, Lonnie Brooks, Left Hand Frank, or Johnny Embury, all waiting to sit in with Hound Dog.

When Wes Race and I recorded them, we did our best to create the atmosphere of one of those club gigs in the sterile environment of Sound Studios. We couldn't bring in all their friends and fans, but we did bring in the same battered amps, cranked them up to the same maximum volume, poured the whiskey, and the band cut the same songs they played every Sunday at Florence's. Because they wouldn't rehearse and hated to play the same song twice, we cut albums in two nights, recording twenty songs a night and choosing among the best takes for the albums. We cut 'Hound Dog Taylor and the

HouseRockers' in 1971 and 'Natural Boogie' in 1973, and the songs on 'Genuine Houserocking Music' were recorded and mixed at the same sessions.

After the release of their first album, their three lives changed dramatically. They went on the road, first to Midwest clubs, then to New England colleges, then to New York concert halls, and finally even to Australia and New Zealand. They established fanatical followings in college-town clubs like the Kove in Kent, Ohio and Joe's Place in Cambridge (where they often played six nights a week for three weeks straight to packed houses, and an unknown acoustic guitarist named George Thorogood opened the shows). They gave three fantastically successful performances at the Ann Arbor Blues Festivals and headlined festivals in Miami, Washington and Buffalo. They played Philharmonic Hall in New York, the Auditorium in Chicago, and literally hundreds of other gigs around the country. *Rolling Stone* printed a feature on them. They even appeared on nationwide Canadian early morning television (where Hound Dog told everyone how happy he was to be visiting the home of Canadian Club).

When I think back on the four years I managed, booked, recorded, drove and carried equipment for Hound Dog Taylor and the HouseRockers, dozens of incidents crowd into my mind:

•Hound Dog shaking the sleeping Ted Harvey after seven or eight hundred miles on the road, and commanding him to 'wake up and argue!'

•The delight of the band in locating a Kentucky Fried Chicken outlet in Melbourne, after they had decided the were going to starve to death rather than eat Australian food.

•A late night slide-guitar duel to the death with JB Hutto at Alice's Revisited in Chicago, with no clear-cut winner.

•Hound Dogs pride at being introduced by BB King to the audience at the posh London House night club.

• Ted falling asleep in a huge shipping carton backstage before a crucial concert and being found only seconds before showtime.

• Hound Dog sitting up all night in a Toronto hotel room with the lights, TV and radio on, because he was afraid to go to sleep and have another one of his dreams about being chased by wolves.

• Phillips stepping in to save me from a knife wielding drunk outside of Florence's.

• And Hound Dog, dying in his hospital bed, desperately hanging on to life until Phillips finally relented and came to visit him and put to rest their most serious (and violent) argument. Brothers indeed.

Hound Dog died on December 17, 1975.

Phillips and Ted still live in the same building on the South Side, (though they are usually feuding and don't speak very much... just like a lot of good friends). Ted regularly plays with Jimmy Rogers and has become sort of the dean of old style blues drummers in town, since the deaths of Odie Payne and Fred Below and the virtual retirement of SP Leary. Phillips still sits in now and then, and recently toured Sweden as guest of the Hjalmar Kings – a sort of Hound Dog tribute band (pretty good, too). I don't think they visit Hound Dog's widow Freda very much these days, but I stay in touch with her, and (of course) she gets his royalties.

When they do speak, Phillips and Ted talk about Hound Dog and his music, as do thousands of fans. But Hound Dog said it best himself — 'When I die, they'll say, he couldn't play shit, but he sure made it sound good!'

'Woke up this morning — I didn't have the blues, but I was extremely worried about things!'

# 8
# Daevid Allen
## ...on the promo/emo-tional history of Gong.

Gong was born as a band in 1969, and by 1992 had made over forty albums. An anathema to some, a total enigma to others, it has always been an 'eccentric alternative', virtually unknown to the public at large. For true Gong freaks, however, this band and its rather odd music and lyrics is much more than a bunch of people playing music.

For example, amongst many other things, Gong is a luminous green planet from a far distant solar system that according to Gong Cosmologists will only be discovered when its envoys arrive in AD2032.

Credibility stretch?? ...well, hang in there!

For me, Gong symbolises that irrepressible lightness of being that defies logic, survives by miracles and lives on beyond cynicism, pessimism and despair. The Foole in the Tarot. Meanwhile for the brave at heart who are prepared to plunge through the 'mirrors of embarrassment' and divine the codes, there is a whole system you can use to 'lively up yr life with holy hilarity!'

Gong is a band but it is also a lifestyle, a politic, a philosophy & a cosmology.

Q: Are we serious?

A: 'Its all much too serious to be serious about!'

Gong's story probably began in Melbourne in 1958, when I was a young maverick artist and jazz musician 'an' then man, *um*, like I 'ad a vision y'know...?' So I left Australia and started on a path that led me through the beatnik years as a Performance Artist and Beat Poet in Paris and London, to the beginnings of the Hippy revolution, and the visions that led to the creation of the Soft Machine band.

I founded Gong in 1968 with my partner, the feminist, poet, and spiritsinger Gilli Smyth. We saw Gong as a spiritual path in the field of popular public performance. The time was ripe. The music scene in the late sixties was wide open to innovation and experiment. For the first time in the history of popular music, music-biz executives had temporarily lost the plot. The power lay in the hands of the 'artistes' and Gilli and I intended to take full advantage.

Gong's international 'band/family' lived communally in an abandoned hunting lodge in a forest near Paris until signed by Virgin Records UK in 1972, and then the community moved to a farm near Oxford. My somewhat unorthodox methods – such as quitting whenever I felt the integrity of the band was threatened by its spreading fame – made me unpopular with the rock business establishment, so I dealt mainly with rebel labels such as BYG Records in Paris, run by the notorious Jean Karakos, and his protege, Jean Luc Young of Charly Records in London.

When I first met Richard Branson, Virgin Records was just being set up and Gong was only their second signing. Still the idealistic London University student, Branson soon put his developing business genius to work on making intelligent rock music commercially viable. In seeking to raise the quality of pop and rock music, we became his willing accomplices. The problem was that BYG records was now bankrupt and Karakos had gone underground, so if Gong were to survive, they had no choice but to sign with Virgin before their contract with BYG expired. Virgin issued the Gong LP, 'Camembert Electrique', paid for by the defunct BYG, for the price of a single and publicised it with full page ads in the London music papers. Within two weeks the album was near the top of the English album charts, and Gong successfully began to tour large venues in the UK. Over the next two years, the Gong LP Trilogy was completed, and commercially the band was going from strength to strength,

Two weeks after the third album was released, BYG records sued Virgin for signing Gong while still contracted to BYG. The legal battle that followed cost Gong all its royalties for the Virgin releases.

By now Gilli had given birth to our two sons, Taliesin and Orlando, and despite her valiant efforts to continue touring, she had retired to be a full time mother. Gilli was irreplaceable and the feminine power she focussed was sorely missed.

I began to feel that, as the audience for the band grew, an extra self discipline was needed. To honour this responsibility to the expanding Gong following, I felt a balance had to be kept between spiritual clarity and drug use.

As the pressures of touring and public visibility intensified, I believed that the original positive purpose of the band was in danger of being overwhelmed. I saw increasing evidence of negative energies using the openness created by drug excesses to take control of audiences. I resolved to stop smoking dope and taking hallucinogens and three of the other musicians agreed to join me.

A schism soon formed in the group and synthesiser wizard Tim Blake led the resistance. By the spring of 1974 the conflict between Tim and myself had polarised into a psychic battle of extremes, and eventually Tim was forced out of the group. Less than a month later, I was prevented (by a mysterious force field) from going on stage before a concert and, exhausted, I retired from the band, leaving Steve Hillage to fill my role of unleader.

As Gong continued without me, I moved with Gilli and my two sons back to Deya in Majorca where more visions resulted in two solo acoustic albums: 'Good Morning' and 'Now Is The Happiest Time Of Your Life' ...anticipating by many years the New Age Troubadour movement. Following a peace-making and spectacular Gong Family Reunion in Paris in '77, I joined with the Here & Now band to create Planet Gong and initiated the now legendary Floating Anarchy Tours. Travelling to the USA, I then combined with Bill Laswell's Material to form New York Gong, touring the USA, managed by Giorgio Gomelski.

By this time my fourteen year domestic relationship with Gilli had ended. Leaving three different Gong bands flourishing in Europe, I moved to New York with my new lover, Maggie Brown. We survived by trail-blazing an alternative rebel circuit for Rick Chafen across the States, playing solo with backing tapes and calling this show Divided Alien Clockwork Band. It was now 1981, and suffering from severe career burnout, I left the US for a seven year retreat in my native Australia, where Maggie gave birth to my third son Toby.

I drove a taxi and worked with the Street Poets in Melbourne, studied New Age Therapies in Byron Bay and lived for a time in a Mystery School in Southern Queensland. After a painful separation from Maggie, followed by a powerful vision during the Harmonic Convergence in 1987, I helped reactivate The Invisible Opera Company of Tibet as an Australian band featuring singer songwriter Russell Hibbs.

By 1988, I was an agile and animated fifty year old. I returned to London with my new lover and creative partner, Wandana. Together we ran Self Initiation Workshops for Gongfreaks and sewed the seeds firstly for the English Invisible Opera Company band and then for the predominantly acoustic cross-cultural Gongmaison. Following an explosive separation with Wandana in 1990, 'Gong: Live On TV' was recorded at

Central TV studios and the Gong of the Shapeshifter era gradually began to take ...er... shape.

In 1991, The Space Agency was created by Keith Bailey and Steve Bates to tour manage the Gong bands and with an updated Here & Now band, the Planet Gong/Floating Anarchy Tours were temporarily revived. I formed Magick Brothers with Mark Robson of Kangaroo Moon as a vehicle for my Celtic acoustic and New Age material. Finally, a Performance Art solo show called Twelve Selves has slowly evolved and simplified into my current solo show which, at the time of writing, is about to make its fifth tour in two years.

Meanwhile, an autobiographical book called 'Gong Dreaming' is due out any time now, and it promises to reveal the 'secret visions and esoteric origins' of Gong, together with an intimate view of my early days with Soft Machine. This will be followed in '95 by Book Two ('95) by further private revelations and a very personal view of my days in the Gong community in France and the UK. On the 8th and 9th of October 1994, Gong will celebrate its 25th birthday with two ten hour festivals, at which most of the various styles of music that the Gong name has embraced and inspired over the years will be represented.

A commercially insular tribe, I suppose we have made it easy for the conservative music-biz to bounce off the superficial psychedelic tag and dismiss the various Gong bands as a bunch of dope-addled woolly-hatted dinosaurs. But how many 25 year-old bands are there in the world that, under the guise of psychedelic rock, have publicly explored such a variety of different musical forms as Gong? Pop, jazz, Indian classical, Tibetan, Arab, Polynesian, rock, jazz-rock, modern classical, punk, New Age, folk, electro-acoustic, techno, rap, performance art, performance poetry, and electronic music?

I'm proud that Gong has survived for the past fifteen of its twenty five years in glorious defiance of accepted music biz attitudes & strategies. We continue to flourish uncompromised by large scale label input, private patronage or royalty cheques from past efforts, and we have been largely unaided by sympathetic press coverage.

How do we get away with it? Search me, cobber.

# 9

# Laura Connelly

## ...writes from her adopted home and says: 'It's an LA thing, man'.

Los Angeles: the new Eden, the new Jerusalem, the new Babylon. Lotus Land, La La Land, autopia. With all its nicknames and guises, the City of Angels is a weird and wonderful place, a city of extremes. There is no consensus as to its advantages or disadvantages, as all of the musicians I've interviewed since I've been here will testify. On the the one hand this is the land of the bikini and the surf board, bordered with beaches all along its west coast; on the other, it's the land of the hiking boot and beard, fringed with the desert and mountains to the east. At its heart lies an urban sprawl of some forty cities, and a population of thirteen million, predominantly made up of migrants from South America, Asia, the Middle East and Eastern Europe.

George Martin, gentleman and producer of the Beatles, notes one important point about LA from his many visits:

'It's a load of suburbs looking for a centre, isn't it? And there's nowhere,' he says.

Some say LA needs no centre, because at its heart is a culture of nonstop movement. Connecting the suburbs are freeways, the umbilical chords of LA life. It's a city of wheels, and in 1940 there were more cars in the city than people. Ask any Angeleno directions and it'll be explained in terms of time and routes not miles.

'The freeway is like a big octopus arm. We probably put more money and effort into that than we do in to any of our endeavours. Well, that's a theory for ten seconds,' say Geggy Tah, two young men, recently signed to David Byrne's Luaka Bop label. They play Californian world music and sing a song called 'LA Lulljah'.

As there is no MOT inspection for vehicles in the state of California, you'll find plenty of virtually written-off jalopies, as well as a healthy handful of Porches on the roads. It's also the perfect locale for Harley Davidson's, as Gilby Clarke, guitarist with Guns N' Roses well knows:

'I have three motorbikes - two Harley's and a dirt bike which I wiped-out on. This is the place for Harleys,' he says .

Nevertheless, there are some LA residents who haven't enjoyed the city's growth in transport.

'It's getting just awful. There are too many cars on the streets, ' says Ry Cooder, who was born, raised and fermented in the LA suburb of Santa Monica.

They've also called LA the first experimental space colony. A wide range of architecture, from the Googie-style coffee shops to Frank Gehry's futuristic designs for the new Disney Concert Hall, certainly make it look that way. Little is permanent, however, and LA has been famous for demolishing much of it's own heritage – not to mention that floored by the earthquakes. As Geggy Tah explain:

'LA is getting old fast. It's new, but it's not built to last.'

LA's main industry is film, and many residents are obsessed with the bright lights of Hollywood. Stretch limos are a dime-a-dozen, and schmoozing with the stars is as easy as bumping into them in the bookstore or the supermarket. It's a place that abounds with vacuous narcissism, kitsch and tackiness. One spin-off of the motion picture industry is that LA is also home to a plethora of musicians, ranging from musicians with the Philharmonic to members of Mexican Mariachi bands. It's the place where MOR rock abounds, yet every taste from rap to African music is catered for. Ultimately it's the place to see and be seen if you're an aspiring muso, and of course, the place to sign that all-important record deal.

Big names rub shoulders with lesser known bands as they pass through on their way to Japan or Europe. The venues are many and varied, ranging from the huge Pasedena Rose Bowl (where the Stones performed on their Voodoo tour) to the relatively minor Jack's Sugar Shack, where the little known surf guitarist Dick Dale can be found. For some, like Ry Cooder, LA is the only place to be if you're a musician:

'I wouldn't take a job if it wasn't in LA. LA is transitory but if you're working here, then you're here and your life is here. We all kind of cling to this little belt of free space out by the ocean, but there isn't any other place to go. If I'm going to work, I'm probably going to be here. In the music business it's best to be here. It's the resource centre, it's where all the musicians are, God knows.'

Branford Marsalis, jazz saxophonist and band leader for the 'Tonight Show', is a New Orleans native who has lived in Los Angeles for nearly two years. He has an equal enthusiasm for the music scene in LA... well, certain parts of it, anyway:

'LA is a place where there is clearly a lack of substance. But there is also substance here. Placido Domingo is the director of the damn LA Opera. Esa Pekka Salonen is the director of the Symphony and the music has been incredible, except no one goes. And the people who do go, go because they want to seem cultural. So they go and they snooze through it. No people my age or younger go. So when you talk about LA, they're constantly interviewing movie stars and pop stars, and most of them don't have shit to say about nothing.'

Sam Philips, female songwriter, born and raised in Los Angeles, agrees:

'Not many good musicians have come from Southern California, there are too many distractions.'

Too many distractions includes plastic surgery, for example. Boob jobs, tummy tucks, penile extensions, liposuction, fat removal, there's no end to how you can change your outward appearance in this Town. There's no secret about it either: the clinics advertise every week in the *LA Weekly* listings magazine. One well known subscriber to the world of cosmetic scalpel sculpture is rock chick Cher, who recently dropped in on George Martin at his hotel to discuss the possibilities of him producing her new album.

'Plastic surgery doesn't turn me on. I'm too old a dog to worry about those sort of things,' he says. 'I like people who are natural, who behave naturally. It's difficult to be that in show business. It's such a seducer of people and particularly in the acting profession and the music profession. Success is a heavy wand to have, some people get their heads turned around. Silly really, because everybody's human and I don't have a great deal of respect for people who do change, who become pompous and arrogant.'

What about Cher?

'She looks jolly good, I can tell you that. She looks absolutely terrific and she's a very happy woman too. I take people exactly as I find them. In Cher's case, I think she's admirable, I really do. '

There's a price to pay for all this luxury, however. Severe fires, earthquakes, the Rodney King riot, as well as an alarming number of residents without car insurance, renders Los Angeles a risky place to live. Although it, surprisingly, does not rank as the city with the highest numbers of murders per year, it is still plagued by crime.

It's the home of the Bloods and the Crips, as well as a myriad of Asian and Mexican street gangs who shoot it out over territory and drugs at least once a week. But the violence is not just restricted to the poor ghettos of East LA and South Central. Since the '92 riots, the stars have been getting jumpy and those who weren't already armed are doing so. The Beverly Hills Gun Club, for example, has had more clients than ever since the uprising.

Ben Harper, young blues/hip-hop songsmith, acoustic lap-guitarist and Hollywood resident, wasn't surprised when the riots happened:

'It was about time. The police have been jumping on us ever since there's been organised law. It wasn't a just result and I don't think what happened with the trucker was a just result. See, it's all a symbol of the decline of justice. It's a continuing decline of justice. All the rapists get off and rape again, it's almost worthless at times. And it frustrates me that what happened they called it a riot, but the riot was when they beat up poor Rodney, that was the riot. And when they declared them innocent, that was a declaration of war and the riot afterwards was a response to that declaration.

'It's been happening for years. I've been jumped on by the police, my brothers have been jumped on by the police. It's not the first time it's happened. It's going on every single day, even as we speak. It's just a part of the continual inequality in education, employment and protection. '

Speaking in his swanky record company office in suburban Encino, hardcore West Coast rapper Ice Cube offers a solution to the problems of the ghetto: 'well, being in South Central, when you're in a poor community and people think you've got money, it's just like being in a group of lions. When one lion gets the meat everybody wants the meat, y'know what I'm saying? My philosophy is, I got the meat, I'm going to make sure of my family and then I'll show all the other people how I'll distribute it. If all the people are drowning I can help them better if I'm on the boat than if I'm in the water. It's rough. It's not about "I'm staying in my community to show how black I am." Showing how black you are nowadays can get your family kidnapped when you're on the road and I ain't having that.

'It's just like anybody making money. It's not the problem that you've moved out, it's when you go and you never look back. It's just for security reasons that I'm out of Los Angeles. You know, when you've got people pulling up to your house that you don't even know, and they want you to come out and sign an autograph, that's basically not cool. I can deal with it when I'm there but when I'm on the road, thinking about my wife and my kid in that situation, I don't know who's friend and who's foe, you know what I'm saying? I know it's just reality, that poverty and frustration brings on crime. And I know it can happen to me. I know I'm not immune to it so what I do is take my family out of that situation and try to get everybody up out of that.'

Opinion may be divided about LA generally, but one thing that everyone agrees on is the weather. JJ Cale, mumbling blues guitarist and Branford Marsalis, at least:

'LA is not my cup of tea. It's okay, but I'm walking around in shorts in January and it's three degrees in New York,' says Marsalis.

'I like those sunny days. That's all you got,' Cale agrees 'Being a musician, it's real easy to get depressed. There's a lot of lows tryin' to play music. I lived in Tennessee, like near Nashville for ten years, and it's really cloudy there. Southern California and Florida are the two sunniest places, I think. I lived in Florida too, but in the summer it's so hot and sticky. Here it's just warm and sunny, it's not s-t-i-c-k-y. So now you know why I'm here.'

Me too.

# 10
# John B Spencer

## ... a short story:

### 'The New People'

To us it will always be Mrs Lee's.

The corner shop.

Out the back.

Despite what they've done to it...

Knocked out the front.

Breeze block.

Neo-Georgian windows.

Pine panelled door with a brass knocker.

'Desirable terraced residence... Bedford Park Boundary.'

You can always tell when a place used to be a shop.

Don't the people who moved in know that?

****

Mrs Lee was very touched by all the 'Good Luck' cards she received when she told us she was moving.

Closing the shop.

'Sentimentality,' she said.

She told us she was moving out of London because of all the car burglar alarms that kept going off in the night.

Not because of the Sainsbury's...

...that had just opened up off the High Road.

Or because Mr Lee had recently died.

Proud woman, Mrs Lee.

My wife took a photograph of her standing outside her shop just before she left. Sent a print on to her, in Shropshire, where she had got a job making floral displays.

You just couldn't imagine Mrs Lee living in Shropshire.

Making floral displays.

****

When my wife asked Mrs Lee what she would be doing when she moved to Shropshire, Mrs Lee had said:

'Floristry.'

My wife misheard her.

Thought she said:

'Forestry.'

That was even harder to imagine.

Mrs Lee with a chain saw.

****

Mr and Mrs Lee came from some island in the Indian Ocean.

We think.

They weren't Indian.

Or Chinese.

Bit of a mixture, really.

Very short, though.

Both of them.

Mrs Lee had a key ring with a picture of a young oriental-looking girl on it.

My wife asked her, once.

It had been puzzling her for ages.

'Is that your mother, when she was younger?'

Mrs Lee laughed.

That, in itself, was very rare.

Mrs Lee.

Laughing.

'Oh, no, dear,' she said.

'That's Helen Shapiro.'

Helen Shapiro was a singer who had some hit records in the early sixties, when she was still a schoolgirl.

Now, she's a jazz singer.

**\*\*\*\***

Twenty years, we'd been going to Mrs Lee's.

Out through the back garden gate.

For odds and ends we'd forgotten from down the High Road.

Milk.

Biscuits.

(When we sent the kids over, they always came back with fig rolls.)

Loaves of bread.

Or to buy things that were too heavy to carry all that way back.

Like four pounds of potatoes.

Mrs Lee ran a good shop.

Lots of variety.

Though I must say...

... her vegetables were never up to much.

**\*\*\*\***

Twenty years.

That's a long time to be seeing somebody practically every day –

She was closed on Sundays.

– and not get to know them very well.

**\*\*\*\***

Apart from on rare occasions, like when her husband died –

Cancer,

'He enjoyed his game of cards.

Enjoyed his drink in the evening.'

– Mrs Lee never said anything.

Apart from:

'Anything else?'

In a sing-song voice.

Before she rang up the total on the cash register.

'No, that's it, I think.'

We used to say.

**\*\*\*\***

Quiet old stick.

Mr Lee –

I suppose that's why we called it:

Mrs Lee's.

And not:

Mr Lee's.

Even though he was in the shop as much as she was.

Until he became ill.

**\*\*\*\***

It must have been weeks before we realised nobody had seen Mr Lee around in the shop.

Bringing out bags of coke from the back.

Re-arranging things in the freezer.

When my wife asked after him, Mrs Lee said:

'He's not himself at the moment.'

Then:

'Anything else?'

**\*\*\*\***

We saw Mrs Lee, once, down Charing Cross Hospital.

She must have been visiting Mr Lee.

Before we knew he had cancer.

That was the only time we ever saw her away from the shop.

In twenty years.

Climbing into a Morris Minor.

We didn't know she had a car.

Didn't even know she could drive.

'That must be why the eldest daughter has come back.'

My wife said.

'To help out in the shop.'

Apart from the eldest daughter, Mrs Lee had another daughter, still at school, and a son who talked to himself when he was walking down the road.

He couldn't have been much help.

We never knew Mr Lee had cancer.

Till after he was dead.

**\*\*\*\***

Peter.

That was the son's name.

Not the full shilling.

Like they say.

Once, I was waiting behind a young girl, at the till.

She had whispered something to Peter.

'Eh?' Peter said.

Cupping a hand to his ear.

In an exaggerated fashion.

The girl whispered again.

Peter turned towards the door at the back.

'TAMPODS!' he shouted.

'MUM! DO WE HAVE ANY TAMPODS? '

Mrs Lee came out drying her hands on a towel.

'Oh, Peter,' she said.

Peter was about eighteen.

The girl about twelve.

I expect she will remember that moment for the rest of her life.

**\*\*\*\***

What I remember is this.

For once, Mrs Lee didn't ask:

'Anything else?'

Before ringing up the total on her cash register.

**\*\*\*\***

Mr Lee came back out to work in the shop for just one day.

The week before he died.

We all thought he was on the mend.

**\*\*\*\***

The new people who have moved into Mrs Lee's have very loud voices and two daughters.

Sophie.

And Sonia.

The husband takes them off to private school every morning in his car.

'Do sit in that seat properly, Sonia!'

'Sophie, I won't tell you again.'

But, he will.

He always does.

Every morning.

****

I say:

'The new people.'

But, they've been there...

At Mrs Lee's.

... a year, now.

Young Dennis, from four doors down, has broken in and stolen their video recorder three times, already.

The third time, they caught him red-handed, walking out the door with it.

Grabbed hold of him.

Dragged him back inside.

Called the police.

Dot, Dennis's mother, went mad at them.

You wouldn't want to get on the wrong side of Dot.

Not if you could help it.

Besides...

...you could see her point.

She already had one son inside and another run over and killed while escaping protective custody.

That's how the local paper put it.

The Brentford & Chiswick.

Protective Custody.

**\*\*\*\***

We all saw the place being converted.

From Mrs Lee's...

...to a desirable terraced residence.

Bedford Park Boundary.

'Right bunch of cowboys,' our son said.

And he should know.

In the trade himself.

'Gerry built!'

He would have said.

If he was older.

We all know what they paid.

To the development company who bought the shop from Mrs Lee.

Twenty thousand over the odds.

And they're crying blue murder over a video tape recorder.

You have to laugh.

**\*\*\*\***

When Mrs Lee used to catch young Dennis stealing buns from the shop she always threatened to call the police.

But she never did.

She wasn't just passing through .

Like the new people.

# 11
# JON RONSON
## ...on Pop Awards.

ere at Ally Pally – at 'The Brits' media room, a squalid, tiny hole jam packed with frenzied stringers – questions and answers are being volleyed around like a tennis game between the Care Bears. If there was any more complicity between journalist and subject, they'd be cutting straight to the post-coital cigarette.

Not that, of course, any investigative probing of 'Two-eyes-one-patch' Gabrielle or Tori 'I'm a dolphin' Amos would trigger an especially scintillating discourse. But still, it'd be nice to hear a line of questioning SLIGHTLY more inquisitive than:

'Gabrielle. What does your boyfriend do for a living?'

'Don't want to talk about it.'

'Oh, go on.'

'Runs a fast food restaurant.'

'McDonald's?' I yell.

'No,' says Gabrielle.

'Burger King?' shouts Rick Sky from the *Daily Mirror*, smelling a scoop.

'No,' says Gabrielle.

'Wimpy?' I shriek, warming to my theme. 'Kentucky Fried Chicken? Wendy's?'

'No, no,' says Gabrielle.

There is a long, long pause, in which everyone tries to

think of something to say. And finally: 'McTuckys?' (Silence). 'It's McTuckys!' I yell, triumphantly. 'We've GOT her!'

Well, a man's got to pass the time somehow. And because we journos have been herded into a tiny room miles from the action, it's an uphill struggle to keep our spirits alive. Celebrities are delivered to us at fifteen minute intervals, we flagellate ourselves wildly for a bit, and they're sequestered again, back to the thrilling land that lies beyond the press room.

The glittering prize of the night is a ticket to the after-show party, where there's free salmon, Tori 'I'm a blade of grass' Amos, and John McCarthy, whose appearance here amongst the drag queens and pre-teen sensations is a wholly weird coup. ('And the next award will be presented by Simon Weisenthal and the Fresh Prince Of Bel Air'.)

The winner of the much hyped Brits vs Brats battle – I am proud to be one of the very few to have attended both – has become, I'm afraid, a forgone conclusion with the appearance of this celebrated radiator-hugger. Had the *NME* dumped Bikini Kill and got in, say, Stephen Hawking to announce Best Male Vocalist, there'd still be a contest.

Furthermore, in employing an appalling, balding, power-crazed asshole to distribute the after-show invitations, the Brits have pulled off a *coup de gras*. There's more than a sniff of the school bully at work in his methods: awarding tickets to those he deems suitable. He refuses, for instance to reward the *Smash Hits* journo with a ticket until she admits that she's over-weight.

'I'll give a fucking ticket to who I fucking want to,' he says to me, when I interview him on the subject. It is rare – a breath of fresh air – to witness a twat of these dimensions at work, now that the pop world is all Huggy-Lovey Boy Next Door. It's nice to know that there are still cunts in the industry, and not just vegans. Well done, Brits!

Of course, it's all bluff and double bluff. One has to create a sense of mystique and privilege, or the whole thing crashes around your feet. What differentiates Kylie from other short Antipodeans is that you have to be derided and insulted before you get to breathe her air. Yes: security maketh celebrity. And minions maketh mogul. When I finally make it to the Brits party, a mighty and prominent rock and roll manager corners me, clicks his fingers, a youngster scuttles over, and he proclaims: 'Give Jon some drugs.' The whole experience is terribly depressing in one respect, and not at all depressing in another.

Somehow, security has failed, and the party is invaded by a horde of screaming fans (the screaming and the frostbite is the only way to distinguish them from this year's crop of teen-sensations: the stars here appear to have been plucked at random). I follow a group of youngsters as they scurry around the tables, attempting to locate Take That. Behind us, security are catching up. One of the youngsters gives up, and is ejected. On the way out, I ask her why she gave in so easily. 'I thought it would be different in there,' she explains. 'But it's all fat businessmen.' It is a sad moment, witnessing this coming of age: I guess you grow up when you no longer mistake the grinding of commerce for the dazzling beguilement.

The party is becoming somewhat dull now, so I pass the time by childishly listing – on a Brits napkin – the things I dislike most about pop journalists:

1. Their perpetual craving to refer to everything musical as being 'orgasmic'. This can only make one assume that they've never actually HAD an orgasm. I, for one, have never been able to identify similarities between the ejaculation of my semen and a Bjork album track.

2. The same goes for 'cathedrals of sound'.

3. And 'shimmering'.

The list isn't going so well – I guess it is a gut thing – so, even though Jason Orange from Take That has just hovered mistily into view, I head off to take a look at the fans. It's freezing outside, snowing, and clusters of youngsters are bunched up to keep warm, screaming maniacally every time a limousine drives past, screaming, then saying: 'who was that, then?'

And as I watch, a teenage girl in a wheelchair hurtles towards me, screeching to a halt inches away from my feet.

'Have you got a pass?' she blurts through the crowd.

'Yes,' I reply.

'I'm in a wheelchair,' she shouts. 'I'm waiting for a heart and lung transplant. Could you introduce me to East 17?'

I glance around at the anxious security guards, eyeing us suspiciously, waiting to pounce, and say: 'I'm sorry. I can't.' And I begin to head away, inside, away from the sleet.

'I haven't got long to live,' she continues, yelling after me. 'And I've got the documents to prove it.'

And then, her final, pleading, desperate shot: 'My lips are bleeding,' she screams. 'My lips are bleeding.'

**** 

I head indoors, feeling a bit guilty about the whole thing. I WOULD have passed her my extra ticket – got her inside – but I couldn't forget a terrible incident that had occurred two years previously, the result of which made me vow never to behave philanthropically towards pop-music fans again. I'd been covering a Cliff Richard press conference at the London Docklands Arena, an awfully stagnant *Hello!*-esque occasion:

JOURNO: 'Do you drink wine?'

CLIFF: 'I have a couple of glasses before my dinner.'

JOURNO: 'What's so special about this tour?'

CLIFF: 'All my tours are special to my fans.' (And on and on.)

So I went outside to collect my thoughts, and I saw a young, tattered blonde girl slumped in the corner of the car-park, crying.

'What's wrong?' I asked.

'I came all the way from Milton Keynes and they won't let me in,' she sobbed.

'The bastards,' I said. 'Why not?'

'They say I'm a danger,' she continued. 'They say I must be kept away from Cliff because I'm a danger to his safety.'

'Why?' I gasped.

'Because,' she replied sheepishly, 'I caused a bit of trouble at his house a few months ago.' She paused. 'They KNOW I won't cause any trouble to Cliff. They KNOW I love him.'

'The FOOLS,' I replied. 'Who do they think they are?'

'I don't blame Cliff,' she added sharply. 'Cliff was always Number One.'

'What makes him Number One?' I asked.

'He's the best looking,' she replied. 'He's both sexy AND cute and he's got the best voice AND the best backing band.' She paused.

'He said in 1965 that he prefers a reserved girl who doesn't like to do all the talking and I'M reserved and I don't like to do all the talking.'

'You sound perfect for him,' I said.

'Well, it's difficult,' she replied, 'because he doesn't like pushy girls, so all I do is stand there and hope he notices me.'

'Well there's no harm in THAT,' I said.

'Can YOU get me in?' she asked, eyeing my press pass. 'PLEASE?'

I looked behind me. There were few security guards about, and I'd noticed a secluded, unguarded fire exit by the toilets. And hell: what harm could it do? She only wanted to STAND there. It wasn't as if she was going to do all the talking. So I headed inside, and round to the fire exit. I opened the door and she rushed in past me, not even glancing in my direction, and hurled herself to the front of the stage where Cliff was performing an acoustic set for the benefit of the journalists.

'Cliff,' she screamed. 'Its ME! LOOK! LYDIA!'

Cliff was doing 'Miss You Nights' at this point, and glanced down, perturbed slightly by the scene.

'Cliff, Cliff,' yelled Lydia, jumping up and down. 'It's me, LOOK.'

But Cliff looked right through her. And then, suddenly, Lydia stopped, hung her head low, and shuffled to the back of the auditorium, tears in her eyes.

'What's wrong?' I asked. 'Why so sad?'

'Look at how I behaved,' she sobbed. 'Cliff likes reserved girls. and now I've totally ruined it.'

'I'm sorry,' I said.

And we both stood there in silence for a second. And then, with the assistance of three large security guards, Lydia and I left The Building.

**\*\*\*\***

So I'm not prepared to go through that again, and back at the Brits, when the party finally begins, I notice a man (who I believe is Dire Straits' Manager) holding court, telling anecdotes, with a rapt group crowded around him. I join them just as he says the words 'package deduction', and a huge laugh erupts from the group. Curiosity overwhelms me. What possible joke could end with the punchline 'package deduction' and elicit such a magnificent. response? I turn to the man standing next to me.

'Oh,' he sniggers, barely concealing his mirth. 'We were talking about product being transferred over the airwaves without any specific format, and he said that we should ask for a package deduction.' He beams.

The terrible thing about cliches – of course – is that they're invariably true, and here I am, sharing a room with the cast of 'Breaking Glass' – fifty-year-olds in pony tails, screeching into their mobiles, telling New York 'no', holding Tokyo. 'Okay,' reply their secretaries from the next seat. And in Tokyo, one assumes, everyone stops what they're doing and just stands there.

And it isn't long before I engage myself in conversation with Bob from something called XFG.

'Tell me,' I ask, 'how many units have you shifted?'

'40,000 units,' replies Bob. 'But we've got a great point share, and Denmark's looking great.'

'Denmark always does,' I say. 'How about Norway?'

'Great,' says Bob. 'Norway's great, but we put Sweden on hold.'

'That's the best thing to do with Sweden,' I agree. 'I held Sweden for a while, but I had to let them go because they got fidgety.'

'Yeah,' says Bob. 'I know what you mean.'

And so on.

They say that the pop industry is just like any other business, but I can't imagine a group of wood-stain manufacturers hailing themselves with such vigour: working in the morning, celebrating each other until bed time. The whole award process fills me with confusion too. Most people make do with a stable relationship, or a night in the pub, but it takes a neurotic of Kafkaesque proportions to have his desperate, avaricious thirst for vindication quenched only by the applause of millions, a name written huge.

But that's the music industry for you. On my way to the toilet, I overhear a showbiz type pontificating wildly towards his companion, saying: 'There's a cliche about A&R men that we're all creative talents forced into dealing with finances.' Really? I'd heard a completely different cliche. That certainly wasn't the cliche I'd heard.

They say we're young and we don't know — we'll find out before we grow...... babe.....

Sunni Muslim ......and CHER.....

# 12
# Mary Costello

...recalls how 'comedians and other musicians' indirectly helped her become a BBC radio presenter.

It has long being a source of amazement to me that seemingly unrelated incidents combine to change one's destiny. It's almost as if life is a huge jigsaw with some of the pieces falling easily into place, and others stubbornly refusing to join in. For example, I am frequently asked how I began working in radio. A simple and straightforward question perhaps, but one with an answer that is not quite so clear cut.

I had been a mother and housewife since the age of nineteen, and the very notion of presenting a radio programme and playing a mix of my favourite music for a couple of hours every week, was the closest I could imagine to heaven on earth. But as far as I was concerned, it was a totally unachievable goal, and I never mentioned the idea to anyone. I had never even been inside a radio station, let alone knew anyone involved with one. So I compiled cassettes for friends and family, purely for my own enjoyment, and left it at that.

It really all began when I mentioned to the bass player of an 'extremely well-regarded R&B combo' that as a bass player he would make a very good comedian. No offense was

intended by that remark, nor was any taken. In fact it transpired that he rather relished the idea of exploring the funny
side of his character, which was rather limited by playing bass
in an 'extremely well-regarded R&B combo'.

So we decided that he should prepare a full routine and
that he would make his comedy début at the Edinburgh Fringe
Festival. We had no doubts at all that he would be ecstatically
received, and that the whole enterprise would result in fame
and fortune all round. So I duly booked a venue for the duration of the Festival and waited for my 'discovery' to get his act
together – as they say.

Within quite a short time, it was becoming increasingly
obvious that as a comedian, he made a far better bass player.
Entrepreneur and Discovery parted company (quite amicably,
of course), but by this time I was committed to presenting
something – anything – for several weeks at the Edinburgh
Fringe Festival. But what?

I didn't have to be a nuclear physicist to arrive at the
simple solution that the easiest way out of my predicament was
to put on a programme of live music. So, along with a promoter
who was already running a regular club night at the venue, and
who agreed to share the risk and any profits (this turned out to
be his first big mistake), I set about booking the bands. For
some obscure reason – which I suspect was a combination of
beginner's luck and sheer naivety – quite a strong bill emerged.
Names like Richard Thompson, Martin Stephenson And The
Daintees, Clive Gregson, and a wild and wonderful Scottish
band called The Screamin' Nobodies (sadly no more, but they
definitely should have ended up as Somebodies) were booked.

So far, so good – except for one minor detail. Up to that
point, I had absolutely no experience whatsoever in promoting
live music. After much thought, I decided that a dry run was
called for. So I found a suitable room underneath a pub in central London and set about booking some bands for a month or

so of Thursday nights. The first night was a major success, largely due to my imminent birthday and to a spot of quick-thinking.

In an unguarded moment, a rather well-known singer/songwriter had asked me what I would like for a birthday present. So, on the first Thursday of my dry run he appeared as special guest, under the pseudonym of the Pope of Pop. Needless to say, his true identity was discovered with alarming – if not totally surprising – speed, and at five-thirty on the day of the gig, a rather large queue had formed at the entrance to the venue. A pity that the doors weren't even due to open until ten.

I was looking after things at the door of the gig when I happened to recognise one of the punters as being a highly respected broadcaster and general arbiter-of-good-musical-taste around town. After this first meeting we kept in sporadic touch. I wasn't to know at the time that this chance encounter was to largely contribute to my being approached, some three years later, for a job as presenter at Greater London Radio. Another piece of the jigsaw falls in to place.

I returned from Edinburgh, exhausted and convinced that I never ever wanted to sit through another soundcheck for as long as I lived. Artistically it was a great success, financially a total disaster. It was a truly weird and wonderful experience, but one which I am in no great hurry to repeat. After a suitable period of recuperation (a month in bed), life gradually began to return to normal.

From time to time I bumped into the 'esteemed broad-caster', which was hardly surprising, seeing as how we shared a love of great music. We invariably found ourselves attending the same concerts, often babbling excitedly over a pint or two, comparing notes about some artist or record without whom the rest of the world could never ever experience total fulfilment or true happiness. It was on one of these occasions that I was introduced to a former producer of 'The Old Grey Whistle Test', one Trevor Dann. And so thereafter *our* paths were destined to cross in similar fashion. It was quite a while after our first meeting that I learned that Trevor had been appointed programme controller for GLR, a new radio station, poised to rise from the ashes of BBC Radio London.

At the time I was totally unaware of events in radio – it was a world far removed from my own – so it came as a tremendous shock when I received a telephone call from the recently-appointed Programme Controller of said radio station. My first thought was that the call was a wind-up. I told him as much, adding that I thought the joke was in rather poor taste. Trevor assured me that he was indeed who he claimed to be, and would I please join him at the radio station for a meeting? I didn't need a lot more encouragement.

As I arrived at the GLR offices in Marylebone High Street later that week, I happened to recognise Slim Gaillard – old Voot-a-Roony himself – strolling by, and naturally assumed that this must be an omen of some sort. In fact, all it really indicated was that the late, great Slim lived nearby. Another theory bit the dust.

I got the job, anyway.

# 13
# Vince Power

**...tells how a hobby turned in to a compulsion and eventually made him a major player in the live music scene.**

At the time of writing, The Mean Fiddler group runs a total of nine venues in London. We put on several outdoor festivals every year – including Reading, Phoenix and the Fleadhs – and professional racing punter Barney Curley has even named a horse after us. But when I first started the Mean Fiddler in 1982, I just wanted a place I could go to at weekends to listen to some good music. The rest came about through a series of chance encounters, luck – some of it bad – and plenty of hard work.

I first came to England from Waterford when I was sixteen. I started out by working as a floorwalker in Woolworths, before being elevated to the post of bedding salesman at Whiteleys of Bayswater. But the retail trade wasn't really my cup of tea, and I tried my hand at several jobs – including building and demolition – before having a go at buying and selling used furniture. This was something I really seemed to have a knack for, and in true Arthur Daley fashion, I worked out of a lock-up garage for a while, before setting-up shop in rented premises on the Harrow Road.

My success seemed to stem from a combination of gut-instinct, sweat and good luck. I once found an old Dutch painting in Kenton, and although I had absolutely no idea what it was worth, I shelled out £10 for it. I returned to the shop and put the painting in the window. During the course of the afternoon there was a steady procession of local dealers coming round and offering me ever increasing amounts of money for it. If I'd have been offered £70 straight off, I would have taken it like a shot, but the first one offered £200, and by the end of the day it was up to £500.

By this time, it had occurred to me that perhaps I ought to get an expert appraisal. So I took the painting to Sotheby's who said that it was old and Dutch, and quite valuable; it later sold in auction for £7,000. That money really set me up in the furniture business and I opened up another shop in Cricklewood from the proceeds.

Eventually I got fed up with the second-hand business and branched out in to new furniture. I was even more successful at that. I was buying up bankrupt stock and mail-order cancellations, going up to places like Manchester and Liverpool, buying wagon loads of anything that would sell. I leased premises on a temporary basis, and at any one time I would have around ten shops on the go.

By about 1980 I was really bored with the furniture business. I had reached a plateau, and it had ceased to be a challenge. I was already heavily into music, and in particular the country and Irish kind. I would fly to Nashville on record-buying trips, and I put on occasional parties over the shop in Harrow Road. This gave me the idea for a club, which I envisaged at the time as a sort of western-style honky-tonk. And that's really how the Mean Fiddler came about.

One night I was watching television and skimming through the *Evening News* when an advert in the paper caught my eye. It was for a club 'with great potential' in NW10. I rang the number and a man told me that it was Terry Downes' old club in Harlesden High Street. I went down to view it that same night, and when I got there they were mopping up the floor. The guy told me that they'd just had a leak, but it turned out that the place didn't even have a roof on it. They would come in and mop the rain water off the floor every night before they opened up.

Downes sold me the leasehold, subject to licence. But I didn't realise that he had already had problems with the law, and that they had actually closed him down. When I went to court to get a liquor licence, the police thought I was fronting for him, and they wouldn't transfer the licence over to me. The only way I could get it was by buying the freehold of the club outright. So that's what I had to do.

I finally got the licence and the Mean Fiddler started from there. My initial plan was that it would be a good-time, good-country bar, serving ice-cold beers and putting on great entertainment. I intended it to be more of a hobby than a business. I had no intention of getting rid of the furniture shops, but as I got further in to the music, I became more more and more involved in the Club.

I lost a lot of money in the the first eighteen months at the Mean Fiddler. As far as I was concerned, it was a country music club, and that was it. I was very single-minded about that and I didn't listen to anybody's opinions. People would come in and say 'if I was you...', but I refused to listen to them, I'd just tell them to fuck off.

We used to have our own Texas-style dancers and a house band. I auditioned every member of the band personally, and I wouldn't rest until we'd got the best fiddle player in town, the best singer, and so on. They used to play every night, regardless of who else was on the bill. We tried to get American country bands to play at the Fiddler, but there just weren't enough of them to go round. Generally we would feature

English, Irish and Scottish acts, although I did discover that the Scots were generally best.

For two nights a week – at weekends – it worked really well. We'd get a lot of airforce base people coming in regularly, and there'd be a great party atmosphere. A typical Saturday night at the time would include the Texas dancers (who used to do a routine on Top Of The Pops when they weren't with us), and I had a choreographer who put together a couple of routines. They used to do a 'Best Little Whore House In Texas' routine at midnight ,and all the men used to rush forward to the front of the stage, leaving the women fuming at the bar.

That went on for about six months, and eventually I had to sell all my other businesses to keep the Fiddler afloat. I finally realised that if I kept slavishly to the country thing, it was going to break me. So I looked around for other types of music to put on.

I used to have a country DJ called Dave Cox, who was very good at his job. He lived and breathed country music, and wouldn't have anything to do with any other kind. The first non-country band I had on were The Pogues. It was a Friday night, and there were about three hundred people in, but half were there to see The Pogues, and half were my regular country fans. After watching The Pogues' set with a look of sheer horror on his face, Dave sidled up to the microphone and made an announcement: 'if this is country music, I'm off'. And he walked out, never to be seen again. Some people clapped and some booed, but that was the end of it. I'd made my decision and I had to stick with it.

I originally put on bands like The Boothill Foottappers, The Shillelagh Sisters and people from America like Los Lobos and Flaco Jiminez. I also moved quite strongly into the Irish scene and booked acts such as Moving Hearts and Stockton's Wing. Once I had opened up the Fiddler for different types of music, people discovered that they liked going there, bands found that they enjoyed playing there, and the whole thing just took off.

By 1984 I was making money, and before long I was making a lot of money. I started getting myself organised and opened up an office, getting Dave-id Phillips in to help me book the bands and run the thing professionally.

The great thing about the Mean Fiddler is that it always keeps you on your toes. You can never relax, because you've always got to work harder than everybody else to get people to Harlesden. If it was situated in the centre of Camden, it'd be easy.

Once I'd got the Fiddler up and running, I got restless again and went off looking for other venues. The Fiddler was fine, but there wasn't an awful lot more I could do with it. The Powerhaus came next, then Subterania, followed by the Jazz Cafe, The Grand, and eventually The Forum and The Garage.

My involvement in the Reading Festival began early in 1989. Harold Pendleton had lost a lot a lot of money at the previous year's Festival, and his company hadn't been able to pay people. Basically they were in deep trouble and he was desperately looking for someone to back him. But Reading had become what I call an 'agent's festival': agent's would ring up and virtually put the bill together to suit their own acts. It had become lumbered with an out-dated image centred around people like Meat Loaf and Bonnie Tyler.

I think I was Harold's last resort after he'd tried all the usual people like Derek Block and Harvey Goldsmith. He telephoned me one day and I arranged to meet him at the Festival site. I'd never ever been to a rock festival in my life, but he asked whether I'd be interested in going in with him and I said, 'yes, why not?' Nothing ventured...

What Harold really needed was someone to front it for him, because no one in the business would deal with him after the previous year's disaster. So we agreed to become partners on a 50/50 split, with the Mean Fiddler fronting up the money. We shook hands on it, and Dave-id Phillips and I went back to the office and took a long hard look at the situation.

We decided to quite dramatically change the way Reading was run. For instance, in those days the VIP area was situated in front of the stage. The first 50-60 feet of the arena was cordoned off, and you had the ludicrous situation of all these so-called VIP's swigging champagne in there, and behind them there'd be the paying customers, straining to see what was going on. That was one of the first things to go. There were also people who had been there for years and who were basically dead wood. It was a long hard battle to change things, and we met with plenty of resistance. Although no one realised it, our first Reading Festival was almost called off fifteen times.

In the end we got there, and we made money. But I never had a written agreement with Harold Pendleton: he'd always find some reason not to sign any contract that was put in front of him. Why this was, soon became apparent.

We had three successful years as partners, but after the third year Harold came to me and said that the Mean Fiddler shareholding would have to be reduced. He told me that he didn't need us any more and that he was in a position to run the Reading Festival on his own. I told him that we had an agreement, and that he'd have to stick to it. I reminded him that we'd saved the Festival for him, and that he'd made a lot of money out of us. But he seemed determined to row us out of Reading for good.

Pendleton took most of the agents out to lunch at the Groucho Club, and told them that although Vince Power had booked these bands off you, I'm willing to take over the deal and pay whatever is contracted. The headlining bands that year were Nirvana, Public Enemy and The Wonder Stuff. We'd had a hard job securing them in the first place, and he just stole them off us. As you can imagine, I was not very happy. In fact, I was furious.

Anyway, Pendleton got away with it. Someone, some-where, must have been on my side though, because that year they had the worst weather ever at Reading, and all the tents blew away. But I was so angry about the whole thing, it completely blotted everything else out of my mind. I just couldn't help thinking that people shouldn't be allowed to get away with things like that. I went to all the legal experts who told me that I had a 50/50 chance of winning any legal action. But of course lawyers *always* tell you that, no matter what.

I tried to get a rival festival together in Newbury, which fell apart – I suspect – because someone had spoken to the police. I can't prove anything, but I know that suddenly something happened that made Newbury Council change their minds about the festival very quickly indeed. I did manage to get the Phoenix Festival off the ground, but more on that later.

The main thing Harold had over me at Reading was that he had legally acquired the rights to run the Festival on the site. He was supposed to sign the right over to me on a 50/50 share, but he never did. By pure coincidence, about a year later I was in the Jazz Cafe with someone I knew, and I was telling him my story, about how angry I was about it all. The man I was with said that he knew the owner of the land, and that he'd get me an introduction.

Several weeks later, a guy rang up and said that he was the landowner of the Reading Festival site, and perhaps I would like to go and see him. So I went down and spoke to him, and told him the whole story. He asked me if we had kept any accounts for the Festival, and I told him that of course we had, and I sent them down to him. A little while later, he rang back and said: 'luckily for you, Mr Pendleton has also been screwing us, why don't we talk further?' It turned out that Pendleton was supposed to be paying him a percentage of the Reading gate receipts over and above a certain figure. It seemed that there was a discrepancy between the figures given to the landowner and the audited accounts I held. He then offered to do a deal with me. I said that to stand any chance of putting on a festival, I needed the lease signed within a week.

By coincidence, Pendleton's cheque for the first payment for the site was imminent, and so I was told that if it didn't arrive, his deal would be cancelled on that basis, and that they'd then do one with me. The cheque didn't turn up on time, and the landowner's solicitors wrote to Pendleton, cancelling his arrangement, and citing the amount of money they had calculated was owed to them for previous years. Amazingly, Harold paid up straight away. But his agreement was still terminated.

When I walked out of the landowner's office building with the lease in my hand, it was one of the happiest moments of my life.

But then the battle kicked off in earnest.

I rang Reading Council and told them that I'd bought the rights to stage the Festival, and that I wanted the licence transferred to my name. They didn't believe me. I told them that I had legal documentation and that Pendleton couldn't legally run the Reading Festival.

There was a farm further down from the site that had been used for camping. Pendleton went to the farmer (who didn't have a clue what was going on) and gave him some money in return for permission to use it. He then went to the Council and said that he was going to run a Festival on that site. But what really fucked him up was that people had to pass through a tiny part of my land to get to his 'new site'. It was only a strip about thirty feet wide, but it was big enough.

At the public hearing the local fire officer said that there was insufficient fire access to Pendleton's site, and so I was granted the licence. I went back to the farmer and told him that I didn't really need his field, but that I'd pay him a couple of grand to use it as a camping site. He held out until a few days before the Festival, and then gave in. He told me that he was worried that Harold would try and take him to court, and sure enough Harold did try and take out an injunction on him, but it was thrown out. We'd won.

So in 1993 we had two Festivals on the go at almost the same time: Phoenix and Reading. After all the messing about we didn't have much time to work on Reading, and the tickets didn't go on sale until the end of June. Phoenix's tickets had been out since March, and although it was a very successful Festival on the whole, we did have a small, but infamous, spot of bother.

There were very strict licensing conditions imposed on us for that first Phoenix: we weren't to allow camp fires, and we couldn't keep the arena open after 11pm. In effect this meant that we had to put people to bed an hour before midnight, which not really the sort of thing you expect at a rock festival. We had a bit of a skirmish in the camp-site on the Saturday night, but it was blown up out of all proportion by the *NME*, who for some reason kept the story running for weeks. That was one problem; another were the Travellers.

We'd been talking to the police for months about the Traveller's situation and they kept telling us that they were in total control. They boasted that they had intelligence out and knew exactly where the convoys were at any one time. So, quite unexpectedly, the Travellers turned up at the site at 7pm on the Thursday evening immediately before the Festival. We wouldn't let them in, so they parked their vehicles outside and walked away, leaving about a hundred coaches blocking the traffic in to and out of the site.

I rang the police and said: 'it's happened, the Travellers are here, let's get our plan into operation.' And they said, 'plan? What plan?' I was understandably quite surprised because – at their insistence – we'd been talking to them about it for ages. Eventually the police spokesman rang back and said that he'd had words with the local superintendent, who'd said that we were to let the Travellers in, keep them in a holding area and see what happened.

I said: 'no way am I letting them in. As long as they're out on the street, they're your problem. If I let them in, they become ours.'

That was at 7pm. At 1am I had a bit of a row with the duty police chief who rang and told me not to wait up, they'd decided not to come.

In the meantime, the Travellers had got their solicitor involved and he was trying to negotiate with me. 'They're ordinary citizens, why don't you let them in?' He kept saying. By this time it was 2 o'clock in the morning.

There was no real problem, I told the solicitor. The conditions on the licence stipulated that there were to be no pets allowed on site. I said that I'd let anyone in without a dog, so long as they all produced a ticket. Out of literally dozens of Travellers and their friends, they could only come up with two tickets. So I said: 'fine, no problem. We'll sell you all tickets.' But for some reason they didn't want to know about that. We returned to stalemate.

By four o'clock the next morning, the traffic was trailing back to Cheltenham, and the police came back to me and said: 'right we're decided to help you out now'. So at 5am every policeman in Warwickshire turned up to sort out these Travellers. The police went over to the caravans and started to move one or two of them off the road in a pretty heavy-handed manner. The Travellers saw what was going on and they soon got their act together. They could see that if they didn't move, all their vans were going to get wrecked. So within about thirty minutes they had all gone.

Once they had gone, we were left with a road littered with dozens of cars that people had just abandoned on their way to the Festival. They stretched as far back as Stratford-

Upon-Avon, and to get anywhere you had to zig-zag through all these abandoned vehicles.

There was a public enquiry about the 'trouble', which turned out to be almost of case of the police versus us. The police said that we couldn't control the Festival, and that everything that had gone wrong had been all our fault. But it was obvious that they didn't want the Festival to happen in the first place. At the inquiry they were totally biased against us, but fortunately they hadn't done their homework very well and their evidence was almost always destroyed by our's. The Council were very fair about it; they listened to both sides of the argument before eventually clearing us of blame.

That was 1993. In 1994, we went back for another licence and the police said that they didn't want Phoenix to happen, full-stop. But there were a lot of people who were in favour of the Festival. The traders in Stratford could see the benefit of it, and so we did eventually get our licence. And it had a lot fewer conditions on it than the first one: we could have camp fires, and we could leave the arena open until 2am. We were even granted a bar licence until 1am. So the Council actually went a long way to sorting out the problems of the previous year. And 1994's Festival went off very smoothly.

But I did find it very difficult to book the acts for that second Phoenix. There were a lot of spoiling tactics going on. The grapevine was telling me that people in the business didn't want the Mean Fiddler to run too many festivals. There were cases of well-known promotion companies making fake offers and then withdrawing them at the last minute, just to keep us from getting the acts we wanted. Then there was the aborted Isle Of Wight Festival, which had options on bands right up until the minute it was finally cancelled.

It would be nice to be able to prove to everybody that Phoenix has got a definite future. The potential is definitely there. There is space for it to grow, and Stratford is certainly in the best part of the country, being dead centre and linked to every major motorway. Give it three to five years, and I know that Phoenix it will have become one of Europe's major festivals.

The first Fleadh was held in Finsbury Park on June 2nd, 1990. I'd always had the idea of a one-day Irish festival, but because I'd never been involved in an outdoor event, I'd lacked the confidence to put one on. But the success of that first Reading gave me push I needed. The bill was already formed inside in my head: Christy Moore, Van Morrison, Mary Black, Hothouse Flowers, The Pogues – basically all the big Irish names. It was quite an easy bill to put together, because practically all the bands had played the Fiddler at one time or another.

We got the licence from Haringey Council, no problem. They were really quite into the idea, and there's a huge Irish community in that part of north London. But I remember the police being very suspicious of Fleadh. They weren't happy with the idea of an Irish festival in the first place, and that first year they videotaped the whole thing, had wagon loads of police horses around, and even had policemen hiding in the the bushes. They were just waiting for it all to go off, but of course it never did.

It was a day when I've never seen so many people drink so much. We were completely shocked with the amount of alcohol we sold. My abiding memory of the first Fleadh was of all these forklift trucks going backwards and forwards loaded down with big, tottering palletes of lager. It was as if there was an endless thirst.

It was a great day all round, and although it went very well indeed, in retrospect I can see that we did get a lot of the organisation wrong. We had arranged with London Transport to lay on extra trains to coincide with our curfew at 10.30pm. They made a mistake with the timing, and the extra trains all went off early, completely empty. As a result, the police had something like six or seven thousand people milling around on Seven Sisters Road, with no tubes and no where to go. Quick as a flash, the superintendent got them together and said: 'right, we're going to march to Trafalgar Square.' And off they went. So there's this bizarre sight of thousands of people singing Irish songs, and marching to Trafalgar Square to get their night buses home.

We've also tried our hand at other outdoor events. Because I'd taken on the Jazz Cafe, in 1993 I tried a 'Jazz On A Summer's Day' with Alexander O'Neal at Alexander Palace. It seemed like a good idea at the time, but it lost money. It was a fine day, and it was a totally enjoyable concert to be at, but it was unlike any other festival I've been involved in. The people were a completely different set to the ones we get at other events: they came loaded down with everything but the kitchen sink. They had tables and chairs and some even had wheel-barrows full of stuff. We had our usual signs up saying 'no food or drink to be taken in', but that rule had to go right away, because people were turning up with huge hampers.

Another 'mistake' in '93 was the Fleadh Mór, held at Tramore Racecourse near Waterford. I suppose it was my attempt to 'bring it all back home', being held in the part of Ireland I originally came from. If someone had come to me and said that they were thinking of running a music festival in a sleepy English seaside village like Herne Bay or Walton-on-the-Naze, I'd have said that they were fucking mad. Looking back, that's just what I did with the Fleadh Mór in Ireland. Unfortunately, nobody told me I was mad.

It was a brilliant site, and we put the whole thing together to make a very good weekend indeed. But we could have done with a *few* more people. One journalist wrote in the *Irish Times* that in years to come, everybody will say that they'd been there, much in the same way that 50,000 people say that they were at the famous Sex Pistols gig at the 100 Club (capacity 300). It was a great line-up – Bob Dylan, Van Morrison, Christy Moore, Jerry Lee Lewis, Ray Charles, etc – but at the end of the day it cost half-a-million quid to put on.

It wasn't what you'd call a 'commercial bill'. If it had been put on by a local council with some money to spend (do they exist any more?), it would have been a great line-up. When I went in to town the next day, they treated me like a hero. But, like at all festivals in Ireland, when the town hear that you're putting something on, they set up their own festival to compete with you. A lot of people turn up who never go near the real festival. There were six to ten thousand people in town who never came up the hill to the Fleadh Mór. Good for local trade, but bad for us.

The Irish music business did everything they could to make sure the Fleadh Mór never happened. We got brilliant publicity after the gig, but before the event, we could hardly get any. I couldn't even put a *paid* ad on to Radio 2 FM, the State-owned Irish national pop and rock station. I paid for an ad in the *Sunday World* and another promoter rang up the paper and said 'what the hell are you doing advertising the Fleadh Mór?' And the editor of the *Sunday World* told him: 'because Vince Power paid £5,000 for the page, that's why.' There was a fear among the promoters in Ireland that I was trying to take over their business, which was totally untrue. I just wanted to do the Fleadh Mór and get out.

Unbeknown to me, one Irish promoter was selling tickets for the Fleadh Mór and then he refused to pay for them. He still owes me £8,000 to this day. In Dublin, I can't book a single night at any sizeable venue in town because other promoters won't let them hire to me. If I want to put on gigs in Dublin, I suppose I'll just have to go an buy my own venue.

The idea that I'm some sort of megalomaniac-monster who wants to take over every venue really came about because of the Town & Country Club fiasco. The venue manager, Ollie

Smith, started a campaign to Save The Town & Country, and to be fair, it was a very successful campaign. It did save the T&C, but under new ownership – mine – and under the name of 'The Forum'.

After we took over the T&C, Ollie tried to tell the media that I had broken an arrangement we were meant to have had together. I was supposed to have agreed not to take over the venue, which was just not true. I had one meeting with Ollie and his partner and the up-shot of that meeting was that I said that I wouldn't touch the place if they were going to stay there. I did say, however, that if it were offered to me, or if it came on the market, I'd have to take a commercial decision. I mean, I couldn't just let someone else walk in and take it.

The truth is that Ollie had burned his bridges with Folegate Estates, the landlords, a long time before this. He'd gone behind their backs and got the venue listed by the local council, which had really upset Folegate. There was an understanding that the place would be developed eventually, but that they would still retain a club there. Remember that this was happening in the '80s, when offices were being built left, right and centre.

When Ollie saw that happening, he thought that if he went to Camden Council, got the place listed, and started a press campaign against redevelopment, then he could get Folegate Estates to change their mind. This, I think, was very naive of him. Folegate Estates got very upset, and said that they didn't want to deal with him anymore. I was approached and my stance was that so long as they were definitely out of the picture, then I was interested. I wasn't the only person interested in the venue by any means, but luckily I was the one who managed to get it.

Looking back on everything that's happened in the last twelve or so years, the most harrowing experience I can remember occurred in the run-up to the first Madstock two day mini-festival. We'd pre-sold both gigs, and I was in the restaurant at the Mean Fiddler, having a meal. My assistant, Eileen, asked if it was okay with me for her to take the cash float home, so that she could go straight from there to the site the next morning. As I thought she had about £5,000 in small change, I agreed.

I finished my dinner and went home. The telephone rang the minute I got in, and it was Eileen screeching down the phone at me. She was hysterical – she couldn't cry and she couldn't shout – what came out was about halfway between the two. But the off-shoot of it all was that money had been stolen.

I jumped in the car and drove straight down to her house. I made sure she was okay, and then all I could think of was: 'how much? how much?' I kept saying it over and over again. She finally told me. It wasn't £5,000 at all, it was nearly a *hundred* times that amount, all of it in cash and banker's drafts. Most of it was money to pay the bands with.

We weren't having a good time with Madness, anyway. They had a production manager who was a complete dickhead, and we were having rows with him all the time. The latest installment was over the way they were intending to film the event; we nearly came to blows over that.

So after all this, myself and our Finance Director, Mick O'Keeffe, had to go and explain to Steve Finan, the band's manager, that their fee had been stolen. The band must have thought that this was the Big Sting they'd been waiting all their lives for.

Madness had an American accountant with them – another complete dickhead – and he firmly told me that the band wouldn't go on stage without the money. I was going to cancel the banker's drafts anyway, and so I set about getting the cash together. I went round to every food stall in Finsbury Park, changing cheques, and taking as much cash as they could spare. We emptied every penny out of every till and safe in all our venues, and contacted every club I could think of, changing cheques left right and centre. Eventually we scraped together enough to pay the bands. But that wasn't the end of it.

When the Securicor van finally arrived to pick up all their cash at the end of the night, it broke down right in the middle of the site. It was only a flat tyre, but it took an hour and a half to change it. The staff and I were sitting around sweating, thinking that there was bound to be another ambush: it all fitted. Who ever had heard of an armoured cash van with a flat tyre, anyway? We were even starting to get suspicious of each other.

We went round to the bank first thing on Monday morning to cancel the drafts, but were told that it wasn't *quite* as simple as that. We'd have to get insurance in case the drafts suddenly turned up somewhere. It was supposed to cost around £20,000, but we couldn't find anyone at Lloyds willing to take the risk. Eventually the bank agreed to refund our money, but only after very long time.

I decided to throw myself at the mercy of the top man at Barclays Bank. We told him that we were going to go under unless they released the money within a week. He did give us it in the end, but it was the longest week of my life.

'Progress of a sort – they're calling us hasbeens, already!'

# 14
# Chris Jagger

## ...heads for France for some 'E-rock & E-roll'. (Any resemblance to persons living – or dead – is entirely intentional.)

The boutiques of Cherbourg have been combed *ma cherie* for false nails, but all in vain: none are the size of an Irish spade, and would not therefore fit onto the thumb of Riff, our finger-pickin' good guitarist. The trouble came, as always, from the door of the hired bloody VW bus. You know what happens: you have to slam the thing four times before it will close properly, and – like a hungry piranha – it eventually claimed Riff's fingernail. He was not in a particularly good mood to start with, and afterwards was spotted cutting up a colourful ping-pong ball on the bar of that night's venue.

Aided by some Superglue (which must be pronounced 'SupERglue' in France, else they shake their heads in Gallic non-comprehension), Riff is back on the road to recovery, watched by an admiring barmaid, who has lent him her manicure set.

Meanwhile the main point of the tour – *ie* the *gastromique* intake – will shortly be taking place upstairs at the Cafe Rouge as *Le Patron* caters to every whim of the Egon Ronay Swing Band: *'But of course, no flesh for you, or horsemeat; fish?*

*Bien sur red or white? A biere for you, bifstek and frites, bien cur? Burnt? Yes, no blood, just as the English like it, ah ha...'*

To eat before or after the gig, that is the question. Too long before and everything is closed; then the damn sound-check gets in the way and who wants to play music stuffed to the gills with *foie gras*, canard steaks, *creme bulee*, cheese and coffee? Eat afterwards when you're dog tired and smell like a locker room, and the restaurants have closed... Get the picture? To play real down-home broke-and-hungry blues, I would rec-ommend a diet of bread and water on tour – but would the rhythm section of Biff and Twang go for it? Needing extra calo-ries to make up for the lack of flesh, they have to refuel every three hours, else you are under heavy manners. And woe betide the gas station that doesn't carry a full selection of Linda McCartney Tofu Tasties en route.

It's all very well of course for the singer, Gob, to take the superior attitude, as he chats in casual French to any female coming his way. 'You weren't taught French in secondary mod-ern,' Biff characteristically reminds him, 'an' it ain't spoken much in Lewisham, neither.' So good to be reminded of how things are back home. Not that the lack of *parlez vous* has stopped Biff from scoring on the *entente cordiale* front. It must be something to do with his natural sense of rhythm, the rest conclude. 'Just don't slow down midway through, try to keep on top of it,' is the parting advise from one nameless bounder at the hotel bar.

Question: what does the time 10.30am mean to you? (1) 11am? (2) Anytime between 10.30 and 11.30? (3) An appropriate time to roll over and go back to sleep? (4) 10. 30?

More importantly what does the time mean to the tour manager? Perhaps he *says* 10.30, knowing full well nobody will be there until eleven. That way those band members in the know can slip out for an early walk around the famous cathe-dral, have breakfast, write postcards and be back for, say 11.15, and still be able to moan at the tardy Riff or Scratch. In fact Scratch is always up for breakfast, and with his fiddle and two pairs of socks, ready to move at a trice. After three days a procedure is established with the French tour manager which enables you to take the time, multiply it by five, divide by eight and add 32 to the answer. Thus 'see you in a half hour' becomes 30 x 5 divided by 8 + 32 = 50.75 minutes approximately unless Twang has gone off in the search for more strings or some soft porn.

French time, like naughty knickers, is pretty elastic, so just remember the French *c'est pas grave*, and shrug your shoulders, which means that there could be a revolution anytime. Thus the term 'Soundcheck at 5 pm' denotes that this is the hour you will probably be stuck on the Periferique, circling Paris, and suffering from carbon monoxide poisoning. But no problem: nothing will lull the band into a sense of well-being more than a great soundcheck with an ever-ready eager-beaver at the board catering to every sonic whim. It *may* sound terrific, but just wait till the support band have finished moving everything around, the board has been reset and the soundman had gone a bottle of wine too far. Then as Biff 'n' Riff launch into the first number you realise the monitor mixes have been switched: the guitar is twice the volume it was, and Gob is sounding like Meatloaf without the bat. Cringe, whinge and back to basics. Personally I can manage without damned monitor-mixes when they're so bad Gob does the whole gig looking like Ewan MacColl about to hail a cab. Still no matter how lousy the gig, there are always some moments to savour. The audience might be 'small but enthusiastic', but the new number went down okay, you basked in the hot lights and pretended you were at Madison Square Gardens. At one point there were even half a dozen people dancing.

At The Cricketers in Bordeaux – *mais oui ma cherie*, it really exists complete with myriad pics of Both' and Viv pasted under the bar, quite authentic except that someone called Jim doesn't book 'em – the temperature is so intense that the band are wringing out their shirts offstage at the end of the first set.

Gob got off stage to dance with a girl who looked vaguely attractive but moved as though one leg was in plaster. You thought it was the Brits who couldn't dance? Wrong, they are pretty useless all over Europe, but prettiest in Prague where the bars stay open all night and a three course meal costs £1.50. Great, except you get paid peanuts. But do I digress? Luckily Gob has brought a proper piece of willow out from Blighty and shows the chaps at The Cricketers how to swing the thing, posing with the bat in one hand and a bottle of claret in the other. There is even a street in Bordeaux where you drive on the left. Ah! the simple joys of the Englishman abroad.

The final gruelling mistake is the last gig, a dreadful biker's festival already running five hours late before we arrive. It's stuffed with horrendous Frog bands launching into 12-bars screaming 'e-rock an' e-roll... yeah... let's do it 'e-rock an' e-roll...', while a mad biker rides around the site letting off rockets from the back of his machine. Come back Johnny Halliday all is forgiven.

Of course I knew the bottle of Jack Daniels would be a mistake, what with all the waiting... but, who cares when you finally go on stage at 3.30am? And as we await the balance of dosh from the Eurogagged accounts section of Banque De Frog, we tell ourselves 'next time will be better.'

But we have our doubts.

# 15
# Miles Hunt
## ...'US Tour Muck'.

There is an unfavourably obese woman on teevee. In fact she's repulsively fat and disgracefully stupid. 500lbs. Thirty five and a half fucking stone! She says that she can't stop eating, but finds her life is unbearable as a fat bastard. Isn't the answer simple?

'I can't deal with being this fat, it depresses me so. And when I'm depressed I can't help but eat even more...'

KILL YOURSELF YOU USELESS CUNT! DO IT NOW, DO IT ON NOW, DO IT ON TEEVEE WHERE WE CAN ALL ENJOY IT. YOU POINTLESS BASTARD. DIE! DIE!

Oh God, I hate this place. There seems to be such a higher percentage of noisy, pointless, ugly, ignorant fuck-witted pigs than any other country I've had the misfortune to land myself in.

I slept on the floor of the tour bus last night. Couldn't face making any sort of decision as to when and where to sleep. So I took the easy option of boozing till I lay where I fell. Regretting my rather non-committal stance now though. The spine is murder. I can deal with the hangover, there is almost a sense of pride to that.

Pulled into Salt Lake City a few hour ago. Last night's LA gig was okay. Albeit in the horrific surroundings of the laughably heavy metal Valhalla, The Troubadour Club. I've spent the last hour and a half soaking my tour-filthy clothes in the hotel launderette. Whereupon a 40-odd-year-old woman from Boston rattled onto me for the duration. Complaining that she was stuck in Utah because her flight home was cancelled due to the snow. Fuck my luck. Had to put up with the usual unnecessary questioning and unrequired opinionating that I have come to associate with most Americans. She even had the gall to claim that SHE was shy! Well, my dear woman, I can only say that it most definitely was not me who instigated this onslaught of verbal diarrhoea.

I'm staying in tonight. There is nothing here to interest me. I just ordered room service. My arse is in a shocking state. It's so difficult to find food that will flow freely through the system here. They're meat obsessed.

'Do you have anything on the menu that is not animal based?'

'Heeyyy, sure we do. We got chicken!' beams the vile grin.

Cunt.

Not being vegan, and having a life-long aversion to fruit and vegetables of all kinds, the only alternatives I find generally available are cheese and eggs. The bread is simply sweet white sponge… it goes on. As a result, the bowels are constantly in a state of compression. And the ring-piece is sore beyond belief, the stage sweat creates interesting dry patches all over the body, but these are particularly unwelcome around the arse.

Two days on…

Drove overnight to Minneapolis after the Salt Lake gig. Well, I say overnight, actually it took a full 24 hours. Arrived yesterday evening. I was preparing myself for harsher weather than this. I mean it's fucking cold, but sufferable. I did a phone interview this morning with a noticeably camp lad who addressed me as MR. HUNT throughout. It was horrible, I could barely take it seriously, well not as I ever do.

Mary Anne had sent me a valentine fax message that was good to receive yesterday. It was an uneventful day for me besides that. I spent the whole day on the bus. I was thinking about Bob Jones. He would have been 30 yesterday. I didn't say anything to my travelling partners about it. I don't know if any of them had remembered, but I wasn't going to be the one to remind them. The bus wouldn't have been the right place. Too claustrophobic, too depressing. It was cold, most were hung-over, I know I was. I kept old Bob to myself.

I did try to call Mary Anne by reversing the charges, using a public phone at a truckstop. I carefully explained to the operator that it would more than likely be an answering machine that picked up. That it was MY phone and that I would accept the charges. What I wanted to do was leave a message or – if she was around to get my dear lady wife to pick up when she hears it's me. Again, stressing to the moronic operator that I would need to speak after the tone and that the charges are accepted. When the answering machine did pick it up, my operator says:

'Sir, it's a machine, what would you like to do?'

In-fucking-credible!

'Like I told you, I want to talk to it.'

Idiot!

'We can't let you do that without someone accepting the charges, sir.'

'It's my fucking answering machine, that was my voice you just heard on the bastard tape! I ACCEPT THE CHARGES ON IT'S FUCKING BEHALF!'

'Sir, that's not allowed, we need someone to accept at the other end.'

FOR FUCK'S SAKE!

Then the bitch tries to tell me that I owe her two dollars for the call and could I please deposit the amount into the pay-phone! Naturally I told her to get fucked and continued hurling various expletives at every dumb-looking passer-by until I returned to the bus. I truly despise this cockeyed country at times like this.

Soundcheck is done. The pinball machine in the club has been worn out. And I've bullshitted my way through various teevee, radio and magazine interviews. My next duty was entirely self-serving. Dump time. I cannot stress enough that touring, and my relative happiness therein, depends almost totally on the state of my bowels The bathroom at the club is the usual foul 'club bog'. No backstage facilities have been provided, such is the grandeur of this tour. Such a bog would only ever be made use of when boozed up and in need to dispense with excess fluids. No solids.

This being the situation, I headed out onto the street in search of a Burger King or McDonald's. Arguably the best place to dump in when deprived of home or hotel. I'd never dream of eating in the shit holes, but a great place to leave the dung pile. Much to my horror, Minneanapolis would appear to be the only North American city where the Golden Arches do not instantly smack you in the face. Deprived of the fast food industry's contribution to personal hygiene, I had no choice but to access the lobby bathroom of the nearest hotel. The Radison. Easy, stayed in hundreds of them. Checked the sign above the elevators:

RECEPTION... 4th FLOOR

The elevator was already on the ground floor. Walked right inside. Hit the button marked 4. Exited on Floor 4. The signed marked

BATHROOM

was easy to locate. I could see the door with the picture of the little guy on it, over to the right of where I was standing. Passed the shoe-shine man. Through the door, into the end stall. Coat, hat sweater on the floor. Belt unhooked. Aaaaahhh...
...dumped in piece.

Once done with the necessaries, I washed up and headed straight back to the elevator. The automatic doors slid to a close with seven or eight of us standing inside, all are wrapped up to face the February weather. All but one, a little runt of a security man. Cap down over his brow, starched suit, 35 at a guess.

'Are you a resident in the hotel?'

'Me? No.'

I mean, why fucking lie? I took a shit, nothing to be ashamed of.

'I don't want to see you using that bathroom again'. The other passengers looking quizzically embarrassed.

'Why would I use it again? I've done what I came to do.'

'I said I don't want to catch you in there again.'

'And I said, "Why would I need it again?"'

'Leave the hotel!'

'I'm in the lift, voluntarily heading for the ground floor, what do you think I'm doing?'

The little arse just stood there not wanting to play the Q&A game any longer. Why could anybody be bothered to do that?

'D'ya have a good day at work, honey baby?'

'You betchya sweet cakes, ah made damn sure some limey mofo dint use that rEEception bat'room twice in his goddamn day!'

'Ooh sweet baby o' mine, ah'm so proud o' you.'

Why do these people even bother living. That dense fucking bitch who wouldn't let me call my own phone and accept the charges. Her and the master of the shit-house door. I wish them both the very worst of luck. I should have told them that I know where they park their cars and I'd be waiting for them when they got off work. That would be wonderful. Imagine them both. Their blood pressure rising high till they got off work. Of course I wouldn't need to be there waiting. the idea of ruining their days would more than suffice. How marvellous.

While the shithouse saga was going on, a couple of my touring partners were in a coffee shop down the street. Some gang of kids showed up, pulled out a gun and shot another kid right in front of them. Right there in the mall. Nice place.

I suppose it's only a matter of time before the entire country goes ahead and kills itself. And I'd like a ringside seat.

# 16
# Darren Brown
## ...'Adelita Broc'.

The main bar area of the nightclub was pretty busy already, even though the sonic boom of the immense PA system wasn't due to be fired up for another hour. He'd phoned earlier in the day to see what time the music began and had arrived well in advance to give himself as much time to eavesdrop as possible. He ordered a drink and parked on a tall stool mid-bar enabling him to see a large proportion of what went on behind him. He surreptitiously studied his own face in the mirror behind the optics and ice, sipped at his beer occasionally and concentrated hard.

'So I say no to the Social Chapter, definitely no.'

His ears pinned back and his eyes darted up to the mirror, scanning the people behind him, looking for a face to fit the nasal cockney twang. He noticed by the imitation art-deco clock that in ten minutes or so, he wouldn't be able to hear his own voice, let alone a conversation possibly fifteen feet away. He had to make the connection now. He tilted his head back a few more degrees so he could see over first his right, then his left shoulder. Annoyingly the voice seemed to have settled back down in its place amongst the general hubbub and rhubarb, or had shut up altogether. His curiosity was aroused by the sight of three women sitting at one of the ugly glass and aluminium tables bolted to the floor. None spoke. Transcendental meditation maybe? A brief moment of silence to reflect and contemplate? He thought the two sitting closest together looked more like they'd just deeply inhaled some top grade skunkweed, but in this place that was also as unlikely as hearing someone discuss the Social Chapter. The more probable explanation was that they were dumb-struck and/or awestruck by their companions parting volley from the debate (though he somehow doubted it had been much of a 'debate' at all).

He saw the eyes flitting from shoes to table to wall, he could almost see the brains floundering and flapping in a futile attempt to conjure a sublime coda. He empathised, recalling his early teen years before induction, when the the great put-downs, shut-ups and show-stoppers would always, with depressing regularity, present themselves only when the moment had well and truly passed. Empathy slipped seamlessly to sarcasm as he conjectured that this pair could wait months and nothing more sublime than a Sybil Fawltyesque 'ooh, I know' would arise Excalibur-like from the swamp that passed for an intellect.

He winced at his callousness. He used to enjoy and revel in his feelings of superiority, now he felt ashamed and beat himself up with the guilt. He was fast developing a conscience and could hardly conceal his growing distaste for the job he did. Unfortunately his transformation from a fiercely loyal, savagely gung-ho 'stormtrooper' was too dramatic to go unnoticed. Eyebrows were raised. They did not suspect him yet of being 'turned' or anything so drastic. They preferred to assume he was a little battle fatigued, a few months away from the front line would hopefully see his appetite return.

His transfer to the recruitment division was passed off light-heartedly as a tactical sideways move. His 'special skills and experience' were 'vital to bring a flagging programme back on schedule'. He was not fooled, a healthy cynicism was rapidly developing to replace his ebbing naiveté.

It had to be her.

She looked serene and confident, almost imperious, the queen bee. Extracting a cigarette from a new pack with the nails of her thumb and forefinger, lighting it (a little theatrically) and bellowing smoke at the ceiling. She sat back and basked, gloated even, she obviously enjoyed her work. Only he could see the foulness her cool exterior hid. He saw himself and knew it had to be her.

He'd been recruited when he was very young, late teens, not because he had the correct political stance but precisely because he had none at all. The Agency despised zealots, he later discovered. A loose cannon could possibly do more harm than any socialist infiltrator. If zeal was required they liked to cultivate it themselves in carefully measured and controlled quantities. If he ever had thought about politics in those early days it was only to re-affirm to himself that it had nothing whatsoever to do with his life. It was the dull stuff he never read on page two of the tabloids or the first ten minutes of the TV news that he never listened to. It was fit only for old people with time on their hands and bone-idle intellectuals who'd never done a proper day's work in their lives. He realised now that the governmental policies and attitudes of the day had had a huge effect on his young impressionable mind well before he'd been recruited.

The insidious Messages seemed to give encouragement and blessing to his hedonistic and nihilistic tendencies. He recalled feeling righteous and wholly justified in his obsession for the accrual of personal wealth and possessions. It was in the air, 'It's a jungle out there and only the strongest will survive'. He didn't know where it came from or who'd said it and he didn't much care either. The fact was it appealed to all his base instincts, instincts that were suffocating any compassion and humanity that might be evolving simultaneously. He was a product very much of his time, an Agency child, a Thatcher youth, when he was hungry they fed him all the sweets he

could eat. Now his teeth were rotting in his skull and he needed to puke, badly.

When they'd picked him up in the SU common room at
Guildford Tech, he'd been a relatively blank, virgin canvas (for
their requirements anyway), and he was only too willing to be
penetrated and scrawled upon for the instant rewards they
offered. In the beginning he rather pathetically thought that if
anything he was using them. It was after all just a job, they
didn't own him, he'd walk when he got bored. Way before he
ever got the chance to test his puny theory the mind warping
programme of indoctrination had turned his head around.

They had hooked and fucked him all those years ago
and he knew that when the glamour and fascination completely wore away, like a disinterested lover they would want him to
disappear from their life. No embarrassment, no unpleasant-
ness, a good clean break. They would tolerate a messy divorce
and amicable settlement with as much good grace as they
would tolerate seeing him in the arms of another. Whichever
way he went he was a dead man. There was no way he could
un-think his revulsion for himself and his employers, it was too
powerful, it was, the truth. Sooner or later he would slip up, no
matter how careful or scrupulous he tried to be (the effort was
becoming a great strain) one day he would make a small ele-
mentary error, nothing much, another agent might possibly not
even notice, but to the omniscient controllers it would be incon-
trovertible proof of his complete deterioration. To do your job
well is not enough, skill must be matched by unshakeable
belief that what you're doing is right. he had no idea how he'd
de-programmed himself, become so unstable, but he cursed
them twice as hard for their failure on his behalf, as he cursed
himself for all the acts of complicity he'd perpetrated on theirs.
They had cost him his life whichever way you looked at it.

At first he'd thought to slip away to the Continent or
South America and hide, but with his not inconsiderable appre-

ciation of the power and potency of the Agency and its many far-reaching tentacles he knew he'd he a prisoner for the rest of his life. A lonely ignoble death would probably be a fitting end to such a wasted and wicked life, but it would serve no purpose. He wanted to hurt them back, to bite the hand that fed, even if it meant he would more than likely end up guppy food on the bed of the Thames within days, maybe hours of committing his treachery.

To his knowledge no agent in the field had ever turned or defected in the Agency's whole twenty year history and in optimistic moments he hoped they'd become lax and complacent as a result, but he seldom allowed himself to think about successful escape, time enough for that, once his act of defiance was executed. For now all his mental energies focused on the two-fingered salute he planned to flip his superiors.

It had to be her.

Though there were no photographs kept on file, and only minimal physical ID, one agent could pick another out from a crowd with almost a hundred per cent accuracy given just the additional technical data. He'd also memorised her unusual code name. The recruiting zone she was currently assigned to was small, as all zones were. He'd been scouring the indicated area for eight days now, every leisure facility and outlet had been 'cased' at least once. It was the third time that he'd been to this club as it was singled out for commendation in her most recent field report. He knew the triple asterisk beside its name did not indicate 'cheap beer, warm atmosphere, rad DJs'. It suggested that the clientele were, generally extremely receptive to her particular style of poisonous propaganda.

Her success rate for class C recruitment was impressive to say the least and her method was childishly simple. She targeted the 'don't knows' and 'couldn't give a shit's', leaving aside the voters. Abstainers are entirely more susceptible and almost as vast in number. Just look at the turn-out percentage of any local or national election, if the apathetic could be miraculously mobilised to march under their own banner (maybe the 'politics is dead crap party'), the result would cause genuine bedlam. The image of a lunatic handing back the keys of power to an orderly made him chuckle.

'Not such a terrible thing after all,' he mumbled into the glass at his lips.

The barman nearest eyed him suspiciously then returned his gaze to the slowly-filling pint glass. No doubt he'd made a mental note to check how much the bloke on his own had spent and consumed so far this evening. There was probably a shiny new penny for the employee who could spot a troublemaker or drunk before any damage was done. A nudge, a wink and you could also ingratiate yourself to the hulking 'dickie-bows' on the door, only too pleased to get the opportunity to advertise their qualifications as unsubtly as humanly possible. 'Yep, it's still a jungle out there,' he thought sadly.

To anyone with a modicum of political awareness she came off as an oafish reactionary, mildly offensive but basically harmless, perfect. The centre and left's lack of initiative and ability to politicise the ignorant and insensible, played into the right's hands. Leaving the opposition parties to their attempts at alchemy the Agency went digging for fresh ore. Like a rattling empty can she was kicked from zone to zone, and wherever she went, she dribbled sweet but deadly droplets of bigotry, xenophobia, racism and whatever else was pertinent to effect a swing in public opinion.

She turned mute acceptance and casual indifference into vociferous condemnation or approval. Behind her was always months of meticulous research and study. She moulded the psyche of her new identity and slipped inside. With her congenial, rough-edged familiarity and convincingly dull parochialism, she soon established herself within her new environment. She was careful not to speak down to people, always to them.

She avoided the mistakes of the politicians and party activists, stepping lightly, like a fox in the farmyard at midnight. She arrived with all she needed, breaking it down and feeding it to them in pieces they could easily swallow and digest. She was the brightest star in the whole division and almost certainly bound for promotion soon.

He'd discovered in the course of his routine checks and investigations that the division as a whole was doing mighty fine thank you very much and the programme could hardly be described as 'flagging', quite the reverse. That night alone in his flat he'd swigged from a bottle of vodka and grimly pondered the inference of this information. It was that night too that he decided not to wait meekly for the butchers' axe to fall.

He couldn't hear a word that passed across the table, but they had all become animated again. She looked at her watch, hurriedly drained her glass and half rising, stubbed her cigarette out energetically. He saw with relief that the other two made no indication of leaving. They were younger and he guessed they'd probably come for a dance later on. She was alone and this was the moment of truth, the first time in eight days he'd felt confident about the likelihood of a positive contact. His stomach turned and his bowels loosened a fraction as he watched her tuck her bag under one arm and begin to pick her way through the crowd toward the cloakroom and exit.

It wasn't until a couple of days ago that he'd actually admitted to himself that there was only really one way of snuffing out this burgeoning starlet. He'd toyed first with the possibility of seduction and elopement but he knew he may as well be trying it on with a microwave oven. She was virtually a robot who lived and breathed the Agency, she'd be adequately trained to politely or aggressively rebuff any such advances and side step anything that might distract her from her objectives. In any case his success rate at chatting up girls from a standing start was somewhat less than exemplary, so that idea was consigned to the bin. His second option was exposure to the sympathetic liberal press, but on reflection he suspected that a programme of 'sleeper' infiltration he'd been involved in briefly a couple of years ago was now so well advanced it was probably just below saturation level. No one was immune, from the BBC right down to the giveaway local rags. 'Big Brother' was writing the funnies and devising your crossword puzzles. Paranoia maybe, but when you'd been part of the Agency as long as he had, you realised nothing was beyond the realms of possibility. He'd been personally involved in stunts and subterfuge so outrageous and audacious that he was sure even tricky Dickie Nixon would've been impressed.

And so we come to the last of tonight's contestants. Step up to the mic now luv, don't be shy, tell us your name. He'd never actually needed to eliminate anyone as part of an assignment but all agents were given basic training in weapons and hand to hand combat as part of the apprenticeship. With a short refresher course every twelve months he was, theoretically, adept enough to deal with a termination. He had no firearm but in his breast pocket was a finely sharpened pencil. He did not find the irony of an HB being used to erase amusing in the slightest.

He was genuinely loathe to perpetuate the cycle of violence (physical or psychological) any longer. He knew there was no way he could ever atone or make amends for all the awful things he'd done, all the hardship and misery he'd inflicted over the years. He sought no refuge or comfort from the knowledge that he was the head of the hammer and not the hand that wielded it. His guilt and remorse were matched only by his desire for revenge. Just one solitary tick in the plus column would after all be a miracle of sorts considering what had preceded it. He didn't really believe in God but he found himself thinking about Salvation anyway. The night before last he'd dreamed of hideous slimy demons squatting in the darkness behind him, (he knew the darkness represented his life up to now) ripping tearing and gorging themselves on his soul. He'd taken it as some sort of divine, cryptic question (tell us what happened next luv).

He was hyped up fit to burst. His heart raced and thudded like a fist against his rib cage. He slid mechanically from his stool and slowly but purposefully made his way after her. As he reached the cloakroom the PA thundered into life, he was the only one in the room who didn't register at least a glimmer of stunned surprise, glee or in the case of the employees, world-weary disdain.

The crisp night air jarred him, the clouds had not come to trap the heat of the day and the temperature had plummeted with the setting of the sun. It had a momentary enervating and sobering effect. He stood motionless on the entrance step and listened to his heart easily out-pace the dull guttural throb coming from within the club. The sound of clicking heels on tarmac snapped his attention back on line. Looking to his right he glimpsed her disappearing into the car park, setting off at a trot he gradually slowed when he thought he was within earshot, didn't want to alarm her prematurely. After all there was still a chance that he was wrong. He cursed his luck and wished he could've been a hundred per cent certain before making a move, then there would've been no need to 'call her out' like a gunfighter in the wild west. Near the centre of the car park one of the orange beacons was broken, the dimness had congregated and thickened there and somewhere within the clicking had stopped. He padded almost on tip-toe and held his breath, straining for a sound and a clue to her whereabouts. As stealthily as he could manage he plunged into the spooky orange darkness.

Nothing, silence, she'd vanished. Shit (once), was that relief he felt creeping in through the back door? He was all at once bombarded by conflicting emotions, relief, anger, fear, relief...

'Looking for me?'

He dragged the air into his lungs so fast he wheezed in exclamation as he spun around. She leaned back against the bonnet of a white BMW. He knew from the way those three words were spoken that he'd been right all along. Gone was the cockney chime, replaced by flat, accentless Queen's English. She had surprised him and he felt foolish for allowing her to do so. But what was he so upset about? He still held two aces, more than enough to disarm her far more dramatically than he himself had been. He said it to himself to bolster his confidence; she doesn't know you're an agent and she doesn't know you know she's an agent. Whichever way round you put them, it seemed an unbeatable hand.

He opened his mouth to lay the first card, her code name, but before the first syllable fell she flatly recited his own as if she was reading it from a cue card stamped to his forehead. Shit (twice). He was sure he felt the blood all drain from his face, the roots of his hair stood to attention allowing the chill night breeze to freeze the sweat on his scalp. He was unaware that he gaped moronically like a goldfish, jaw flexing in mimicry of actual speech.

'So what have you got to say for yourself?'

If she had a knockout punch she wasn't delivering it just yet, her voice had brightened, was almost genial. In his confusion and panic he completely failed to detect the sardonic edge to the question. Bolstered by the weakness he thought/hoped he sensed he gathered himself to strike a meaningful retaliatory blow.

'Adelita Broc,' (hoarsely) a cough, then 'Adelita Broc, Recruitment Division,' loud and firm.

His elation lasted only as long as it took for her to make a response, or rather for him to realise she'd made none at all. Not a flicker, not a hint of surprise or even recognition that he'd said anything, at all. To be certain he repeated the four word mantra as authoritatively as he could. She laughed as if he'd just told her a weak joke and made to light a cigarette. When the Zippo 'chinked' and leaped into life he could see her face clearly. She held the lighter up for a few seconds, almost as if she wanted him to see her thin lips slightly distort into a grin, her eyes not smile at all. How they regarded him, cool and cold, unblinking. She lit the cigarette and chuckled as she exhaled the first drag.

'Little behind with the news, aren't we?'

His brow knitted, she was pushing him now, playing with him, jabbing and prodding, wearing him down, willing him to lash out, but before he could counter with some sort of desperate defence she beat him to it, again!

'Promotion,' she spat.

No geniality now, her tone was venomous and hate-filled. One more card to play, he thought, with little conviction. He began to reach for the pencil in his pocket and she mirrored his movement exactly. Instead of seizing the initiative as a professional would've done, he froze and narrowed his eyes to try and glimpse what it was she drew from inside her jacket. She gripped it in her right hand, straightened her arm and slowly raised it level with his face. He whimpered uncontrollably, but still utter disbelief prevented him from dropping to his knees and begging for mercy.

'Adelita Broc, DELETION DIVISION. I got my well-deserved promotion four days ago and you have the honour of being my first completed assignment.'

'Oh shit.' ( Thrice).

He'd been right about at least one thing though, she obviously did enjoy her job!

Somewhere in the distance dawn was heralded at least four hours too early.

*'It's the very latest, man – Rockoco.'*

# 17

# Laura Lee Davies

## ...on Madness.

If it wasn't for Madness, there are members of the band who would probably be in prison now. It's true, ask 'em, they won't deny it. It's not that they're all a bunch of criminals, but certainly guitarist Chris Foreman and sax man Lee Thompson would have been up to something a lot more mischievous on weekday nights all those years ago, if it wasn't for regular appointments with 'Top Of The Pops'.

If it wasn't for Madness, I'd probably be a junior school teacher by now, if only because, until I discovered the pure joy of pop music, I had a disturbing pre-teen fetish for the stationary cupboard in the corner of the classroom...

I turned 13 in 1979. It was a great year for music, the '70s sinking slowly with a distant glitter of glam, a haze of lumbering rock and the abrasive blast of punk all melting into what was conveniently loosely called the New Wave. For some, it was the charms of hard-faced urban swaggering from the likes of The Undertones and The Jam, but even by then I rather felt it was older-brother music, the kind of stuff I could appreciate, but that I'd kind of missed the boat on. All the loose ends were being tied together and the seeds of my own tastes came from all sorts of sources – wacky TV appearances by the likes of Jilted John, birthday gifts of Squeeze singles, the rich and varied pickings of my father's record collection, ranging from Steeleye Span to Steely Dan via The Stranglers and Isaac Hayes, my younger aunties' tastes for The Monkees and The Beatles and the preferences of older girls in my school who insisted that The Boomtown Rats were great because they were good looking (which I found even more difficult to fathom than the appeal of their punk-pop hysteria). I had yet to find night-time Radio One on my dial and I didn't have a clue just how much music was going to be part of my life.

Then along came Two Tone, something which (to me) sounded good, looked good and, most importantly, I could be part of from the beginning. Not being a matching-pencil-case-and-hairgrips kind of a girl, I didn't much care for pin-up pop-stars, even if spiky-haired school-teachers like Sting were the unlikely 'throbs of the day. Gazing upon the brutal sulk of The Specials' Terry Hall and the cheeky-boy looks of Madness' Suggs, sex appeal or lack of it wasn't an issue. Even their songs weren't about lovely ladies made in heaven on hot dates with hunks, they were about dancing, getting pissed and having a laugh. Even the utterly beautiful Pauline Black of The Selecter dressed down in boyish suits and trilbies.

Out of all the Two Tone bands, Madness were the most versatile, the most pop orientated and most detached from the constraints of the latest musical fashion. This was made easier by their mix of glam, punk, soul and pop influences in with the ska sound, the fact that they were from north London, a good few miles from Coventry, and of course, their enduring self-cynical sense of humour, or nuttiness as we had to call it back then.

But it was actually because of my dad that I took my passing enthusiasm further. He'd bought 'The Prince' and I sneaked it out of the house to take it to Heather Lihou's 14th birthday party. It got scratched. To conceal my crime, I thought that if I asked for their first album for Christmas, he'd hear the song being payed somewhere around the house and never wonder where his seven-inch had got to.

I played my first copy of 'One Step Beyond' so many times it wore out. It had a jump on one track and I used to sing along complete with the skip in the track. I remember one Sunday standing in the street with my friend, both of us trying to recite the names of all the members of the band, because they'd all had their pictures with captions included on the black and white cover of 'My Girl'. Oh, and don't forget the semi-permanent Chas Smash.

If Madness had been an East 17, Take That or even Blur kind of a band, there wouldn't have been much worth sticking around for once I'd found out what snogging real people (and not just bedroom posters) was all about. But Madness were like a football team, every one chipping in to write songs, all of them dressing up in ridiculous costumes for their now legendary low-budget videos, each with a strong identifiable charm of their own, beyond different jaw structures and haircuts. If you only knew Madness from their wacky videos, to you Lee Thompson was the one prepared to fly around a playing field in the video for 'Baggy Trousers'. If you really knew what they were on about, a Thompson songwriting credit on a number called 'Embarrassment' had to be something to do with family shame, a song called 'House Of Fun' was much more likely to be about teenage sex than a fairground attraction.

With 'Parklife', Blur finally mastered the *fin de siécle* urban concept album, but they have filled their album with characters and little of their own strange souls. Their songs are collectively written, but with little personal identity. The thing was, Madness really could empty your head and fill it with 'The Return Of The Los Palmas 7' or driving Morris Minors up to Muswell Hill, but they could also write songs about cruelty to animals, American military domination or the Northern Irish Troubles. But they did it without once waving flags or any laboured dialogue, and if you didn't want to hear it, you didn't

have to. Their last 'Top Of The Pops' appearance before split-
ting up (the first time around) was a fitting and graceful exit,
did you notice that they were singing 'Waiting For The Ghost
Train' dressed in suits covered in a design of newspaper head-
lines saying 'Soweto Bloodbath'? Well, their was that moment
of sheer unsubtlety when Chas (Cathal Smyth) Smash wrote a
review of the 'Ragged Trousered Philanthropists' for the band's
magazine circular...

Madness, seven blokes between 17 and twentysome-
thing, art students, fathers and labourers, were growing up.
Their world got bigger as they toured the real world, but
whether they were singing about police with water guns in
Italy or the down and outs of Camden's Arlington House, they
approached everything with great honesty. I can't remember
what the music journalists of the time had to say in their album
reviews. I recall a hundred interviews of a band saying we
want to grow up and a press wishing everything was still
baggy and nutty, but it didn't matter, they were a band having
hit records, they were on the television and radio, they even
made a spoof Radio Two programme cassette for the fan club.

If you were a member of the Madness Information
Service, you got a quarterly comic. The fact that it wasn't a
glossy tribute to the 'dishyness' of the band members and
instead was full of cartoons and lists was typical of the gang
mentality that filtered through to the fans, when we all gathered at their gigs. The first comic included biographic question-
naires with all the members of the band. Alongside unnecessary details about heights and favourite foods, there was a top
ten favourite records. From Eno/Byrne's 'My Life In The Bush
Of Ghosts' to just about everything from Kilburn And The
High Roads, there were dozens of records I'd never heard of.

I know someone who became a mormon because The
Osmonds were. I was completely taken with these records I'd
never heard. If they were anything like my favourite band, I

had to hear them. The fact that they usually turned out to nothing like them – James Blood Ulmer, Roxy Music an' all – in sound, but had an inspiring link in spirit opened up an entirely new world to me. Suddenly the shelves of Our Price record shops beyond the Top Twenty racks seemed to be full of magical old sounds that made pop music make sense. By the time I left school, my mum was despairing of my sprawling record collection and groaning bedroom floorboards. I walked straight into a job going on about records when I left college, so she eventually got the point. Since Madness's post-Greatest Hits return in 1992, I've been the one writing features about them.

I talk to my 13 year old cousin Laura about football because we both support Manchester United, but I'm not so bothered about Take That or Michael Jackson. I guess the fact that I still jump around the room at the thought of a new CD by a Welsh-language indie band from Dyfed means that I'm exactly a normal 28 year old female, but even if Laura doesn't turn into a rabid music journo, I hope pop music has something decent to offer her too. Thing is, I doubt it very much. Ah well, we can't all be into pop music intelligent misfits. Perhaps it's time she heard Pulp...

# 18
# Keith Bailey

## ...recalls one very long, very crazy day on the Here & Now tour bus – aka the mobile Gestalt therapy unit – *circa* 1978

Wooooaaaarrrrashkathump! Another 40-ton artic blasts it's dinosaur passage past the bus, which is left rocking gently in the slipstream. A grey morning pokes cold fingers through my curtain and lays an icy hand on all the bits sticking out from under the duvet. I recoil and assume a foetal position in the forlorn hope of an extra hour, but too late. My curiosity is aroused by a rhythmic chomping sound issuing from the general direction of what we laughingly call 'the kitchen'. I execute a perfect Immelman under the duvet to emerge at the bottom of the bunk, where my sleep-starved eyes are confronted by the awesome spectacle of Grant 'I'm sorry, it's all gone, whatever it is' Showbiz. He is stuffing something black and horrible (which might once have been toast, but is now rendered mercifully anonymous by a three inch coating of what I hope is butter) between a pair of incredibly wide jaws.

Gavin da Blitz, fake keyboard maestro, has also spotted this from his pit, and he performs an immaculate double somersault with pike, which puts him right next to Showbiz, and this possible source of food... But Showbiz is well used to this, and with a grace unexpected in so disease-ridden a body, twists and ducks away from da Blitz's clutching paw. He sprints to the front of the bus, cackling triumphantly. Da Blitz rummages through the wreckage of whatever happened last night, and emerges gleefully brandishing a dry Weetabix of unknown origin, which he smears with butter, and demolishes whole.

My stomach, honed to a razor edge by the alcoholic excesses of the previous night, does a neat double-flip, and crawls whimpering into an unoccupied corner, probably where my liver used to be...

But there's nothing for it, absolutely no chance of any more sleep, despite the muffled whifflings and mutterings all around me. My stomach has bravely re-emerged, and is smashing itself up against my rib-cage with a fierce persistence which will not be denied. Blearily, wearily, I make my way to the front of the bus – head, liver and stomach beating the shit out of each other as I go. Da Blitz looks disgustingly cheerful, but has the good nature to shove a cup of quadruple strength coffee and a Gauloise under my nose. 'Kick-start', he grins, and raises his mug to start the race.

This is how it's done: you take as deep a drag on the Gauloise as you dare, and follow it up with a hit of the coffee, repeat three or four times, and *schlooosch!* Your insides turn to liquefied elephant shit, and it's a desperate sprint for the nearest bog, with Da Blitz either just behind, or a nose in front... Unfortunately, this morning, we are parked in a lay-by somewhere near Liverpool, and there don't appear to be any, uh, *facilities* here, and I don't know if I can keep this together.

Legs and arms strategically crossed, we crawl/roll back to the bus and climb painfully aboard, only to be confronted by a maniacally leering Showbiz, dressed in a gabardine raincoat. And that's ALL...

'Just going flashing, chaps,' he cheerily chortles, and

jumps off the bus to take up a strategic position, from where he starts leaping out in front of innocent commuters, revealing his quite probably diseased dangly bits with screams of insane laughter. The poor unsuspecting drivers probably not quite believing what they're seeing...

I think about a little lie down... It already had all the makings of a crazy day.

When I awake, we're in a traffic jam on the M6. Nothing unusual about that, I think, so decide to risk a quick sortie to the front. Steffi, our guitarist and chanteur, is 'navigating', not that we seem to need much of that, what with three miles of traffic stretching south ahead of us...

'Where are we tonight?' I venture, not being really sure that I want an answer to this one.

'Preston,' comes a slightly mumbled reply. Hold it, hold it, keep calm!

'But we're heading south.'

I manage to keep the rapidly burgeoning snarl out of my voice, but Steffi, in a state of hyper-sensitivity over his abject failure to keep this show on the right road, is aware of every psychic ripple within a 15 mile radius, and reacts – as if under attack from the spiritual mafia – with a deadly cold stare.

'I KNOW', he says, very clearly and slowly, as if speaking to a retarded rhesus monkey. 'We're just waiting to get to the next exit so's we can turn round.' One of those very long pauses gets up and stretches itself, makes a cup of tea, has a cigarette and curls up to sleep in the corner...

'Oh, right,' I manage eventually, deciding to forego the subtle pleasures of asking how we got to be heading south in the first place.

'Look you guys, I really wish you wouldn't skin up till I've done my breathing exercises, I mean I'm choking to death back here!' Kif-Kif, our drummer/vocalist/wind-up-specialist looks a lot worse than I feel, his matted, stringy hair is full of bits of cigarette papers, roaches, and what could be some of last night's dinner. The face beneath is a web of lines of pain and stress. Steffi compassionately takes a huge toke on the spliff and blows the smoke straight into KK's face.

'Oops, sorry man,' he sniggers.

KK, feeling that his fragile dignity is about to be shattered, comes back with what he hopes is a withering counterblast: 'You poor, sick little specimen,' he sneers, 'I suppose I should feel sorry for you, except you'd probably like it.' He wheels round and returns to the back of the bus, honour satisfied, Steffi mystified.

'What's the matter with him?' His aggrieved tones grate on our ears.

'Maybe we should get off the motorway and let him do his stuff' says Gavin helpfully.

'Fat chance!' says Steff, 'we're going to be stuck in this for at least an hour, ' he adds in a tone suggesting that whoever got us into this should be shot, quite forgetting that it was he who...

I take a surreptitious glance at the driver, who looks a bit like one of those opium addicts you see in the kung-fu movies – you know, sort of wrinkled, sweaty and pale. 'You ok?' I venture. He immediately launches into a mumbled resume of last night's abuse, finishing up with a heartfelt plea: 'for god's sake get me a cuppa-tea!'

This is done with remarkable speed, it being the unspoken attitude of the band that anybody crazy enough to be able to handle this mobile lunatic asylum and drive deserves a great deal of respect, not to say reverence, the kind you gave to human sacrifices in the old days, for the year before they were bumped off. . . not too far removed from the reality of this situation, really.

At last, the traffic gets moving, and our driver starts to look vaguely human again. We hit the next exit and turn off, at which point KK resumes his demands for a stop so he can do his breathing exercises. We find a spot by a trunk road and off he goes, running across the fields to escape the traffic fumes.

We know he'll be gone for an hour, so Gavin and I settle down to the serious task of getting some money out of Showbiz, so we can go and get some breakfast.

'Sorry, no, no money, there's none left after all that booze last night.' He tries unsuccessfully to keep the sadistic glee out of his grin; this is his favourite game, making us all suffer for our over-enthusiasm of the night before. 'We've got twenty quid, and that's for diesel up to Preston.'

He is almost beside himself with joy as he sees the look of desperation on our faces, but Da Blitz comes back with a real showbiz-stopper: 'well give us that, and we'll siphon some juice from a truck on the way.' He says it with a calm assurance, which has to be total bullshit.

Showbiz's eyes narrow cunningly: 'and what makes you so sure we'll get a chance to do that?' he replies, with the air of one who has an irresistible argument.

'Just you let me 'n' Keith sort that out,' is Da Blitz's stout reply.

Showbiz now has the look of a man who can see he's lost a battle, but tries one more shot: 'Oh sure, you two are the world's best diesel thieves bar none, I suppose,' he sneers weakly.

But Gav's ready for that one: 'Listen, buddy,' he snarls menacingly, 'I've siphoned more diesel than you've had hot dinners,' which is something I find a little strange, but on he goes: 'Come on, out with it, hand it over!'

Showbiz's hand strays involuntarily towards the pocket where he's stashed the loot – that's enough for Blitz and I, who leap on him and forcibly wrench the dosh out of his pocket, totally immune to his cries of pain and frustration, and sprint off the bus and over to the nearest grocery, before Showbiz has time to recover.

We return, arms full of bread, eggs, cheese, cereal and all manner of goodies. The starving hordes mob us with less than usual restraint, which means we are pummelled and scratched into dropping our precious loads and fleeing while the rest of this scurvy crew stuff their faces... Showbiz leading the attack with the venom which is born of a thwarted dictator robbed of his rulership. Blitz and I, being old hands at this game, set about our secret stash of pasties in peace. Ah, the rewards of a cynical foresight!

Kif-Kif returns from his exercises, and we're back on the road, hoo-bloody-ray, heading in the right direction this time, Steff having been unceremoniously bundled out of the navigator's seat. And wonder of wonders, it's only one o'clock, plenty of time to get to the gig.

Well, you'd think so, wouldn't you?

We're heading up the M6, when a very worried looking Kif-Kif heads up to the front. His girlfriend and *chanteuse*, Suze da Blooz, who is heavily pregnant, has at last gone into labour. It looks pretty serious, and can we pull into the nearest town? It's a place called Nantwich, and we hurtle off the motorway, scattering loose dishes and cups all over the floor as our, by now totally wide-awake, driver stretches our nerves and the bus engine, driving like the total maniac he is, leaving us squirming in unfeigned terror. We stop by the first phone-box we see, but before anyone has time to get off the bus and call an ambulance, we're surrounded by the Old Bill – a meat-wagon in front, a car alongside, and one behind.

We've been doing a 'free' tour, where there's been no admission fee, but a voluntary donation collected halfway through the show each night. It's had a lot of publicity, and we've been making some pretty radical statements to the press. The result of this is that we've been stopped by the 'busies' on the way in to every single town we've played, and – as often as not – on the way out, too. They seem to know all our movements almost before we do, and indeed, the Special Branch have told us that they 'have a file three inches thick on you lot.' So it's no big deal to be stopped like this, it could even be a quick way of getting an ambulance.

A plod with more pips than a grapefruit on his shoulders gets on, and says, in a voice like a strangled donkey, 'good afternoon, boys and girls, Here and Now, isn't it? Well, I think we'll just have you and the bus down the nick, and give it a bit of a turnover, like.'

'That's fine, but Suze da Blooz is in labour, she needs to get to a hospital quickly, any chance of calling an ambulance?'

'Mmm, well, I don't know about that, now, let's just have you all in the van now, and we'll see about it at the station…'

Jesus H. Christ! Where the fuck does this guy get off? Best to go along with him and sort it out at the station…

On arrival, we're all bundled off separately, Suze included, so no-one knows quite what's happening. I ask what they're doing with her, and am told in no uncertain terms to mind my own business. They start a strip-search, waiting 'till I'm starkers, then weighing in with searching questions like 'so you're the tough guy in the band, are you?' With a knee hovering over the ol' delicate bits, what do you say to that?

After about an hour, we're all herded in to a room, with the exception of Suze… 'She's gone to hospital, then?' 'Not 'till after she was strip-searched,' leers a spotty young constable. I manage to catch Kif-Kif before he gets to the jerk, not wanting to lose the drummer on a GBH charge.

Eventually, they finish their fun, and we return to the bus, to find it in a state of absolute mayhem – ie in an even worse state than usual, with blankets and mattresses strewn all over the floor, empty bags scattered everywhere and their contents festooned around the bunks. It looks like a horde of delinquent chimpanzees has been let loose, which is, of course, just about right…

We decide to try and get hold of Suze at the hospital, and wonder of wonders, we are connected straight away. She insists that we go on and do the gig, trouper that she is, and so we go for it. By now it's 4:30pm, and we're going to have to do some very serious motoring. I think about a little lie down…

'Come on, wake up, we're here!'

It's 6:30 pm, and doors open at eight. We have to get the PA in, set it up and soundcheck in an hour and a half… no problem… Just ignore the Social Sec bleating in our ears, and get on with it. And, lo and behold, it is indeed done. Just time for Da Blitz and I to get into our favourite game, namely seeing who can drink the most ale in the shortest possible time and still be able to stand up, not be sick on the stage, and play an immaculate set… Of course, mistakes have been made.

Showbiz arrives backstage to tell us we've got five minutes, and is totally ignored as usual. But after twenty minutes of full-on Showbiz pressure, we cave in and it's five more minutes to the off. Adrenaline kicks in, it's packed out front, and we're pretty knackered. A monster spliff makes the rounds, and within seconds the band is reduced to a semi-hysterical giggling mess. (Hey, that's par for the course!) Showbiz heads up to the mixing desk, time for a quick check on the flies, and we're on…

Two hours later, we come off. They were going apeshit out there, but it's all over now, and the post-gig buzz is really kicking. Gav reaches over me and into my bag, pulling out a can of beer… how well this bastard knows my ways. I grab the can in one hand and his testicles with the other, a tried and trusted manoeuvre under such circumstances, and Da Blitz looks into my eyes long enough to know that I'm deadly serious. Reluctantly he relinquishes his grip. A potentially violent situation is resolved when a smiling student arrives with a tray full of beers, swiftly followed by another, and another, and yet more… until there's no more room for any more in the dressing room.

Da Blitz gets a foxy look on his face, and takes up position behind KK with a full glass, which he tips over his head and chortles 'congratulations dad!' KK looks positively evil, but does nothing until Gav's attention is distracted by the arrival of yet more trays of beer. KK picks a glass up and carefully lobs it, so that it shatters just over Gav's head, showering him with beer and broken glass. Showbiz cackles maniacally and hurls another glass at me, and well, what can I say? The evening ends harmoniously with three inches of beer and broken glass all over the dressing room floor. Da Blitz drunkenly climbs the scaffolding to the DJ's capsule, set on taking over the job, scratches an album as he tries to find a track, and is set upon by the rugby team bouncers, and evicted from the premises with none of the deference and respect due to so fine and sensitive an artist.

Outside, we've got a bit of a problem… the batteries have gone dead on the bus, and it won't start. I think about a little lie down, but fortunately, we're perched on top of a hill so a bump start'll be a doddle. We notice a police car parked at the bottom of the hill, and it's such a narrow road that he'll be blocking us in once we get going, but no matter, we'll deal with that once we've got this fucker started. Off we go then.

'Push harder you wimps!' screams Showbiz happily, being excused such duties, owing to his 'bad back'.

'FUCK OFF!' yells Steffi enthusiastically in reply, as with a lurch and a rumble, the engine roars to life…

'YEEHAAA!' we all shout, our voices dwindling as we realise we've made a small error of judgement, forgetting that once the bus has started, it takes about a minute's running before the air brakes are ready to work. The bus is rolling majestically downhill with NO WAY of stopping before it gets to that police car, which in turn has no chance of getting out of the way.

It really does all happen in slow motion, you know, and it seems that we have all the time in the world to watch these two old bill put Starsky and Hutch to shame, and athletically leap out of their car, before, quite slowly, and very inevitably, our six-ton bus goes KABOTCHKA! straight into the front of their lovely shiny new police car. Total write-off, of course.

It really would have been quite nasty if they'd still been inside, wouldn't it?

Up strolls one of the boys in blue, trying to stop his legs shaking, (the other guy's being sick in the gutter) and utters the immortal words: 'I think you'd better come along with us, pal.' He looks really puzzled at the sight of ten people rolling around having hysterics.

*Soooo*, we get out around 4am, and head straight for the hospital, to be told that Suze has had a little boy... Well, you've got to celebrate, haven't you?

I think about a little lie down...

# 19
# Tom Robinson

## ....lays it on the line for aspiring singer/songwriters.

Why would-be songwriters choose to send tapes to the opposition (ie fellow songwriters like me) rather than to record companies, producers and publishing houses is beyond me. But they do. By the box-full.

Often their songs are really well-written, well-sung and well-produced. But you *know* no fucker is going to buy them in a million years, because they lack packaging. So, to the umpteen aspiring fellow songwriters out there preparing fresh demo tapes to unleash upon an unsuspecting world, I offer the following advice. If it sounds a little harsh, well, get ready for the real world. It's a lot harsher.

Make no mistake: the music industry only ever helps those who help themselves. It's no use waiting for a talent scout from Sony or EMI to wave a magic wand and turn you into a pop sensation overnight, it just doesn't happen. For most of us the only realistic hope is to set about creating a momentum and excitement of our own, quite independently from the music biz or national media. Take the attitude that you're going to make it anyway – if someone chooses to pick up on you and help you on your way, fine – if not, it's their loss. Once you've got a buzz happening around you, the music industry will beat a path to your door in any case. But it will take time.

Whatever happens, you won't suddenly achieve stardom in the first twelve months – it might take twelve years – just ask Chris Rea about that. You must want success enough not to care how long it takes, just so long as you eventually get there. If you're in a hurry, try a different career. Of course, things can happen very rapidly indeed, but never count on it.

Let's take it for granted that you've got ambition and some musical ability – although an excess of the latter can hinder as much as it helps. By far the most important factor in a successful artist's career has to do with identity and focus: in a word, PACKAGING. And this is the one area musicians most often neglect.

The world is full of nice songwriters kitted out with synths or acoustic guitars, scribbling ditties about their love-lives or about social injustices, sitting waiting for the world to discover their talents. But why should anyone come to *your* gigs or buy *your* albums? What's in it for them? Because you play nice music? Because you're a nice person? Forget it.

People choose music like they choose their clothes: to express an identity. Wearing a Happy Mondays T-shirt or Sisters of Mercy badge is a public statement about who you are. Others impress their friends with Pavarotti or Sting CDs at dinner parties, while Billy Bragg carefully packages himself for people who loathe packaging...

There are lots of reasons why people become fans and follow a band – sex, rebellion, snobbery, fashion, loneliness, alienation – sometimes even to show they appreciate great musicianship, though that comes pretty low on the list. Yes, I know you're talented, but nobody's going to care about that until you get this other stuff right first.

The key questions to answer honestly about your music is: who would want it – and why? Don't rely on praise from friends and family. To make it, you have to be able to win and nurture an audience of your own from scratch, whether by making indie singles in a bedroom, or gigging round every pub, club and dive that will have you. The competition is ferocious. Your goal is to become an 'in thing' that people will passionately want to belong to. After all, who's going to spend their last couple of quid on something tame or ordinary?

To stand out from the hundreds of others you *have* to know your target audience and pitch accordingly. This doesn't involve abandoning your principles, just defining them. Most successful artists simply pick an aspect of themselves that's true, simplify it, amplify it and then make music to match – a total package that hits their intended audience between the eyes. Name, clothes, image, attitude, style, lyrics, artwork and music all add up to a clearly defined identity. Be as radical and daring as you like: in fact he more radical and daring than you think you can possibly get away with. Take chances, be risky, get remembered. Actual originality isn't essential – just look at the charts for proof of that – but conviction is. Whatever you do, it has to be very, very real.

Finally, a few important questions to ask yourself:

1. What level of success are you eventually aiming for? The local pub? Marquee? Hammersmith Apollo? Wembley ?

2. What kind of record sales are you eventually aiming for? 500? 5,000? 500,000? 5,000,000?

3. Do you see yourself as the next Take That? Tom Waits? PJ Harvey? Pearl Jam?

Your answers to these questions are vital. Until you get concrete ideas of what you're aiming for, you can't hope to plan a route. If you loathe compromise and sound like The Fall, there's no point choosing the greedy answers. If you're after Prince's crown, sharpen up accordingly.

Oh, and why not limit sending your next demo tape to producers and A&R departments who can actually do something with it? Your fellow artists are probably far too busy packaging their next project to listen with both ears, anyway.

# 20
# Ron Kavana

## ...a semi-fictional extract from his forthcoming book:

### 'Fussy'

There's a story that used to go round at home... When I was a teenager there was this pub at the bottom of Hatchet's Hill known as Ma Geany's. Now if Ma G had ever known anything about personal hygiene, the knowledge had long since deserted her. Not to put too fine a point on it, herself and her ould boozer were downright manky! However, this lack of salubrity did not mean that Ma didn't have her fair share of business, though to be absolutely clear on the matter, it must be said that most of her clientele either shared her hygienic persuasions or were 'Jack Tarred' from every other watering-hole in town.

Now this was in the days of the tapped barrels, before porter was chased along plastic pipes by a jet of gas from the cellar to the bar-top dispenser. In those days your pint of plain came in a regular beer barrel, which sat behind the counter in full view of the Billies. None of this modern how's-yer-father about cellar temperature, coolers, clean pipes, gas pressure or what-have-you. A pint of plain was a pint of plain, was a pint of plain.

Some of the taps on those old barrels were inclined to

leak, and it was standard practice to leave a pint glass under each tap at night to collect any drips of the precious liquid which might otherwise disappear in the night. It was less 'standard' practice, in fact it was frowned on, but nonetheless a fairly common occurrence for this glass of drips (which could be almost full by morning), to be topped up and served to the first customer of the day if he didn't appear too fussy. You must bear in mind that unlike today's gas-driven keg, your pint of plain was still (*ie* virtually flat) beer with a consistency more akin to Northern English ale or other such bitters than the Guinness, Beamish or Murphys as we know them now.

Like most publicans, Ma G made her living mostly from the weekend trade. On the Friday night the more fortunate ones, who had found a bit of work on the QT, would be getting rid of their hard earned bobs with such astonishing determination, you'd think it was blood money or had some such shameful stigma attached. Then the following morning they'd be in need of The Cure. Once The Cure was achieved (as it inevitably and invariably was by these tenacious health freaks), they found themselves over the first, and most daunting hurdle of the marathon Saturday session - the Settling Of The Stomach. By the time the stomach was settled, the porter would be slipping down with a minimum of difficulty, the troubles of the world forgotten, and a serious day's *craic* well and truly under way. The Full Sesh (as my good friend Mulligan refers to it) would commence at opening time, 10:30 am sharp, and continue right through to the stagger-home hour sometime after midnight.

The only other day Ma did business of any account was Tuesday. Tuesday was Mart Day, and the livestock dealers, up to their ears in shite from one end of the day to the other, cared not a whit for Ma G's aforementioned lack of salubrity. But, more relevant to our story, Tuesday was also Dole Day... Every Tuesday the unemployed and supposedly unemployed would line up on the street outside the dole office come rain, sleet or heatwave, until admitted one-by-one to the presence of the dreaded dole officer. The DO's all-knowing, all-seeing scrutiny would be stared down with brazen defiance and feigned indifference and the solemn declaration of 'no work and no prospects of work for the coming week' would be made and duly signed before the anxious out-of-worker could beat his hasty retreat back through the queue, clutching his pittance as relieved as a petty thief who has just gotten away with his first crime.

On the Tuesday in question, one Billy McGinty signed his declaration of self-unemployment, and collected his dole as he had done every Tuesday for as long as anyone could remember. Billy was an honest-to-goodness poor wretch who had never been in any kind of serious trouble that I had ever heard about... he was simply one of life's misfortunate misfits. Born into a large family and not blessed with a particular sharpness of wit, he struggled through school only to leave as soon as legally possible in order to take his place in the eternal dole queue. Aged somewhere between forty-five and sixty years, he was a short stocky man with a short thick neck and a large head which was mostly bald except for tufts of shaggy black hair at the back and sides. He was a cheerful enough sort with a ready smile, never more cheerful than when settling his stomach .

'A pint there, Missus,' called Billy, slapping one of his crisp new ten bob notes on the counter.

'I've just the thing here for ya, Billy,' replied Ma G, reaching for the three quarter full glass of drips which she topped up from the barrel and placed in front of the unsuspecting McGinty.

'Get that down ya there now, Billy, and there'll be no fear of ya.'

With that Billy took the glass in his fist without further

ado, and poured a long deep guzzle of it past his permanently parched lips. Suddenly a look of absolute fear and revulsion came over his face, and with a horrific, demented scream fit to wake the dead he slammed the glass back on the counter...

'AAAAAAAARGH!'

'What the devil ails ya, Billy McGinty, is yer stomach not right?'

'AAAAAAARGH!' once more.

'Sweet mother of God man, have ya taken leave of yer senses?'

What Billy had taken was a firm grip of the counter as if to control his fraught emotions, but he still seemed to be experiencing extreme difficulty in the simple, but essential act of breathing. After several minutes of spitting, gasping, spitting, convulsing and yet more spitting, he finally blurted...

'Jaysus Merciful Saviour Missus, is it trying to kill me ya are?"

'What in the name of all-that's-sacred are ya on about, have ya gone daft or what?'

'I'll tell ya what alright Missus, I'll tell ya what's the fucking matter... there's a rat in me porter, that's what. A dirty great big fuckin' rat, a fuckin' foot long in me fucking pint of fuckin' porter, that's what's fuckin' well wrong.'

And sure enough, there it was – not quite as big as it seemed to poor Billy – but a rat nevertheless, head down in the glass with its brown arse sticking up out of the porter.

'Sure it must have fell in and drowned during the night,' was Ma's somewhat offhand observation as she retrieved the offending glass from the bar.

'I'll sort it out for ya now,' she continued, as she dipped her filthy hand into the glass, took the protruding rat's tail between thumb and index finger, extracted it from the glass, and with a nonchalant flick of the wrist, landed it in the cardboard rubbish box in the corner. Without further explanation, apology, ceremony or comment, she turned to the barrel and topped up the self-same glass for the second time, and replaced it on the counter in front of McGinty whose incredulous expression fully summarised his impression of the appaling sequence of events.

'For pity's sake Missus, yer surely not expectin' me to drink that, are ya?'

'And why ever not?'

'Because just half a minute ago it had a fuckin' rat as long as your arm swimmin' round in it, that's why fuckin' not.'

'D'ya know something Billy McGinty, y'are awful fussy, ya won't drink it with the rat or without it.'

Before we pass on from the subject of rats and being fussy, there's a great old song called 'The Avondhu Boys', which I'm inclined to return to occasionally at gigs and more often at sessions when called upon to sing. I first heard it sung by the great Paddy Tunney and later recorded it with Rob McKahey as a Stump B-side. Strangely enough John Peel took a great shine to our version of 'The Rats' and played the hell out of it on his radio show, but I could never get a Peel session out of it as the record company didn't credit me on the sleeve... Thank you so much Ensign/Chrysalis!

'For fun and diversion we have met together,
I'll tell you from Cork boys, it's hither we came.
We crossed the big ocean in dark, stormy weather,
Our pockets were light and our hearts were the same.
Sad at leavin' old Ireland, but once more on drier land,
By the roadside a tavern I chanced for to spy,
And as I was meltin', my pockets I felt in...
For the price of a drink I was mortally dry.

Oh we are the boys with the fun and the eloquence,
Drinkin' and dancin', and all other joys,
For ructions, destructions, diversions and devilment,

Who can compare with the Avondhu Boys.
In the tavern I rolled, to the landlord I strolled,
Good morra said he and says I – if you please
Will you give me a bed, and then bring me some bread,
And a bottle of porter and a small piece of cheese.
My bread and cheese ended, I then condescended
To seek my repose, so I bade him Good Night,
Soon under the clothes I was tryin to dose,
I first tucked in my toes, then I popped out the light.

Well I wasn't long sleepin', when I heard somethin' creepin',
And gnawin' and chawin' around the bedpost,
My breath I suspended, but the noise never ended,
Said I you have damnable claws for a ghost.
Then to make myself easy, as I felt very lazy,
Over my head I again pulled the clothes,
Yerra Moses what's that, sure a great big jack rat
With one lep from the floor jumped right up to my nose.

So I reached for my hobnails, and gave him a bobtail
And wrastled with rats til the dear light of day,
When the landlord came in and said he with a grin
For your supper and bed, you've five shillings to pay.
Five shillings for what now don't be disgracin' yourself,
Said I to the rogue if you please I can't sleep with these rats
and you've the Devils-own-face on you
To charge me five shillings for dry bread and cheese.

Well the landlord went rearin' and lepin' and tearin',
He smashed in the windows and kicked down the door,
Then when he could go no further, he roared mila murder;
These rats they are eatin' me up by the score.
They sleep in my stable, they eat from my table,
They wrastled my dogs and they killed all my cats.
Then landlord said I, you give me those five shillings,

And I'll tell you a way to get rid of those rats.

So says I to him we'll invite them for supper,
And dry bread and cheese lay before them for sure,
Never mind if they're willin', just charge them five shillings,
And Devil-the-rat will you ever see more.'

THE still, small Voice of Reason.....

"STING!! You pretentious ARSEHOLE!!..."

# 21
# Ivor Biggun

## ...explains how lowly BBC sound engineer Doc Cox came to make records – and have them banned by his employer – and go on to become Esther Rantzen's Right-Hand Man.

It was 1978. Punk had burst its boil, and earnest young men in tight suits were calling their music New Wave. I was thirty two years old, a frustrated howling-at-the-moon boogie hound, with a day job as a BBC sound engineer. In the evenings I trudged the pubs and earned reasonable money in an Old Wave country duo, booked by a piss-artist agent who sent us out as sort of Dolly Baez and Englebert Denver.

One night, standing there in my cable-knit sweater singing 'Leaving on a Jet Plane', it came to me. I'd always wanted to make a record, and spiky-haired herberts with three chords and rips in their pullovers had kicked the business wide open. All I had to do was find something that nobody else was doing, add some swearing and a revolting stage-name, and I'd be in with a chance. A visit to the 'Live Stiffs' show convinced me. There was Ian Dury, swaggering around the stage burping and screaming and being a-bloody-stonishing. And he was even older than me, poor devil.

The following night I was driving home from Shepherd's Bush, and THE IDEA arrived. The chorus hit me in the Goldhawk Road. It came as quickly as an over-excited-merchant-seaman-who-couldn't-find-the-delay-spray. By Acton High Street I'd got the verses, and the middle eight blew in through the window like a dirty chip-paper along Ealing Broadway. As I pulled on the hand-brake outside my little house in Hanwell, my *nom du disque* was there, too.

Do you remember those bogus book-titles that the big lads at school used to snigger about? 'The Pile In The Road' by GG Dunnit, 'The Hungry Baby' by Nora Titsoff? Well, I remembered 'The Happy Bride' by Ivor Biggun, and I dashed inside the house to scribble down his 'Wanker's Song' before I forgot it.

I didn't have a band, and I couldn't afford a studio. However, in my department at The British Broadcorping Castration was a wheezing old three-track recorder from the '60s. Nobody used it at night, and in the pre-Birtian '70s, life at the BBC was very relaxed. So I was able to bring in a guitar, a ukulele and a dreadful old bass with a neck like a guilty giraffe, and begin multi-tracking. Yes folks, this peon of praise to pulling the plonker was simply me... er... playing with myself.

After three nights, I had the finished master and a friendly pervert put it on to the end of a bootleg tape that was circulating. It featured out-takes, famous people using the pro-creative word, and the Troggs having a philosophical discussion about the finer points of rock 'n' roll drumming ('You 'ad it then, you great pranny! It went dubbah-dubbah-dub!') ...and me!

This meant that when I finally cut some acetate discs and sent them to record companies, everybody had already heard the song. But they still wouldn't touch the thing with a double-length asbestos barge pole. Finally, I submitted it to the smallest, seediest record company I could find. They had just scraped a top 40 placing with The Lurkers and were operating from an Earls Court shed with one typewriter and no electricity. They signed me up on a standard form for an advance of five pence (which they didn't have, so they gave me a badge instead).

The record company was Beggar's Banquet, and they signed some no-hoper called Gary Numan the same day. I wonder what became of him? They pressed up five hundred copies of 'The Wanker's Song' and sent one each to people who owed them money. Life is tough, when you're an 'indie'.

A few shops ordered one or two, the music press slaughtered it, and (since it mentioned wanking) it was declared unfit to broadcast. How times change. Nowadays a programme isn't fit for broadcast unless it actually recruits a token wanker. I mean, have you ever watched 'The Word'?

In 1978, though, it really didn't look as though my five knuckle shuffle song was going to set the world on fire. So, Loretta Wynette and me and my cable-knit returned to the pub circuit for a while, and then I went abroad for five weeks holiday.

When I returned home, I couldn't get the door open. It was jammed against telegrams and letters telling me that the record was hotter than a flatulent Mexican with a blowlamp, and I was to appear in one weeks time, bottom of the bill to Stiff Little Fingers, at the Lyceum. The same Lyceum where I'd watched Ian Dury cavorting like Gene Vincent doing a Max Wall impersonation. I was terrified.

I recruited five mates as a vocal group. We stood and watched the Fingers sound-check. They came and talked to us in Ulster accents as impenetrable as gorilla pubes.

The audience, a square mile of denim and leather, stampeded in.

I don't drink much.

I looked at the audience.

I drank a bottle of Lamb's Navy Rum.

I stood in the wings, completely arseholed.

The DJ announced me and I walked to the central microphone. By the time I arrived there I was as sober as a marble wash-basin. Plugged into the Fingers mighty sound-rig, I held in my hand the loudest ukulele in the world. I clouted the strings and launched into a medley of my hit. From nowhere a massive torrent of spit, and a greater selection of vegetables than you'll find in Atlantic Road market, rained down on me. I somehow finished my song, followed it up with an amusing ditty about farting, and then walked off stage dripping with gallons of gob and turnip puree. The man from Beggar's Banquet ran up to me. 'Ivor!' he beamed, 'They loved you!'

Eventually, the record peaked at nineteen in the national charts. It was toppled from number one in the new indie listings by Wayne County and the Electric Chairs with the charmingly titled, 'Fuck Off.'

I recorded my follow-up album in six days for six hundred pounds, in a tiny airless hole in Holloway. After each day-long session I went home and boiled my rancid clothes. Two more albums followed, and a few singles which sniffed around the lower reaches of the charts like a sex-crazed Bedlington Terrier round a well-pissed-on tree.

Finally I thrust my twelve-incher into the hands of a BBC producer, told him that I could write clean material too, and landed a job with Esther Rantzen's 'That's Life!' TV programme. This led to a bizarre few years where I was sound-engineering for the BBC by day, performing masturbatory melodies to drunken bikers by night, and dressing-up as a carrot and chasing people on film at weekends.

And Ah! The Glamourous World of Rock 'n' Roll! One night the Bigguns played the Nashville Room in Fulham's North End Road and, confined to a pongy dressing-room, the band asked where the urinal was. The booker pointed to a flip-top plastic waste bin in the corner and said, 'If it was good enough for her out of Blondie, then it's good enough for you.'

A rugby club engaged me to play a free gig at their Fete. 'We'll put you on in the club-house and charge admission,' the potato-nosed prop-forward assured me. 'Don't worry, we'll keep all the toddlers out.' They did too. I strolled on to the improvised stage, blinded by the single spotlight, and launched into a jaunty audience-participation number called 'I Have A Dog , His name is Rover; When He Shits, He Shits All Over.'

It didn't seem to be going down too well. As my eyes grew accustomed to the light, the cold truth dawned on me. Only the first row were hairy rugger-buggers. Most of the rest of the audience were nuns. In a swift change of gear that took even me by surprise, I found myself launching into a medley of Frankie Vaughan and music-hall songs I didn't realise I knew, played in strange, unexplored keys. I even essayed a brief tap dance.

After what felt like a fortnight, I left the stage to the sound of my own footsteps, pouring with perspiration. 'Sorry about that,' said potato-nose, 'but we had to let 'em in, see? It's difficult to say no to a nun.'

Over the years Ivor has had nude stage invasions, flotillas of inflated condoms drifting over the auditorium like zeppelins, trouserless bikers swinging from the ceiling, interesting suggestions from members of both sexes, a large brown dog singing along, and a rockabilly-type walking on stage and threatening to kill him... er, ...me.

Once, a ferocious feminist with Tampons for earrings screamed 'Rapist!' at me (thus displaying an incomplete knowledge of both feminism and bishop-bashing). Another time, the short one in Bros told me that they used to sing my song on his school bus.

The dreadful ditty follows me round like a smelly old

golden retriever, but I still get a kick out of singing it in the pubs and clubs. With my sweetheart Jilly on sax, and Pete, Nigel and Andy making up a shit-hot-or-what band, we crank it up once a week or so, and it's all good not-very-clean fun. Sometimes we go out as a, er… three-hander with that great rude-reggae man from the '70s, Judge Dread and a wonderfully funny four-piece called Rude Prat.

We're cheap, we bring our own PA, we can get the whole pub rocking with laughter and we're much more fun than Leonard Cohen. Mind you, I once had an attack of piles that was more fun than Leonard Cohen. Thanks to 'Ivor' I've met, and played with, a good number of excellent (and usually thirsty) musicians. For a while some of us formed a loose aggregation who played dirty old Stones-type blues for fun. We called ourselves Ivor's Jivers, and I was happy as a pig in chiffon. Nowadays we sometimes add a fiddle and accordion and go out as a strange lumbering seven-piece and play holes-in-the-underpants country and blues in posh places where people have never heard of Ivor Biggun.

Being a right old tart, I just like playing what middle-aged toss-pots like me want to hear. I'm a really terrible musician. If you were to stamp on Bo Diddley's fingers, he would approximately duplicate my style. But I don't give a fantailed duck. Just give me a thirteen-amp mains socket and a twelve-bar blues, and I'm ready to boogie.

Mind you, sometimes when I'm standing on a coffin-sized stage in a dismal boozer in Plumpstead, duck-walking between the dartboard and the fag-machine, my mind does wander back to the Lyceum. It's 1978. It's show-time. I'm standing in an ocean of phlegm, and I'm holding the loudest ukulele in the world.

# 22
# Roy Harper

## ...'The Shock Of The New Record Business'.

In 1974 the recording industry was pretty much a world leader in terms of (western) worldwide commercially successful leisure industry, and as such it seemed to have unlimited potential growth. That growth is still occurring, even though the structures that were built around it in the '50s, '60s, '70s and '80s, are now largely irrelevant or derelict.

The structures stand there, like looted pyramids. Most of the wealth has long since gone. In 1974 at EMI Manchester Square it was virtually five secretaries per man, and a four inch pile on the carpet. Take a look in there now: virtual decimation.

Most areas of 'the business' have known this for years and have attempted to adjust accordingly, so that the demise of the record industry that 'was' isn't that obvious to the woman in the street. Sure, it becomes a little harder to get more specialist items, but since most people's tastes don't run to much more than a combination of Pavarotti/Gabriel/Madonna/REM/Jackson/Guns/U2 and Garth, then Woolworths can definitely do the job. Throw in Elvis and The Beatles and Asda is the country's A&R department.

The problem with this is that the shelves are poverty-stricken compared with even two years ago. The recession cannot be blamed entirely. There was quite a bit of cash around in the '80s, during which the universality of the more catholic tastes of the previous two decades were considerably eroded.

Much of this was perpetrated and sustained by stupidly negative journalism. As if any of those chiding critics could suddenly turn up at a Killing Joke gig and take over. A lot of these people are failed musicians, and so it stands to reason that they would want to kill a goose that never laid a golden egg for them personally.

At the same time as a vibrant and intelligent critical system is both necessary and healthy, these people have caused great damage to art forms they would insist have inspired them. They have contributed massively to corruptions that have turned young musical talent in other directions in droves.

They seem to have needed to become ringmasters of a 'survival of the fittest' circus where they are the undisputed sole arbiters of what should and what shouldn't be appreciated, and how. They have allowed their opinions to become too subjectively biased.

This I guess is understandable in a world where image is all and the catwalk rules, where visual perception is the most obvious and most abused of the senses. Out of sight, out of mind: Jurassic vision. The easy option, judged to be more important than anything tasted, written, heard, spoken, smelt, sung or touched. Just plain lazy.

However, whilst these thin people have played their part, more dramatic changes with wider implications have been taking place in the real world. Fashion and function. Bigger contributions than all the acts of seedy journalism combined, than any probable recession, than any possible boom, are responsible for the downturn in records (music) sold, for the lack of available diversity, here in the so-called 'west'.

Awareness of each other would be at the top of my list – together with the rapid growth of other leisure industries – though everyone's list would …well, perm any nine from the Reading guest list. In there somewhere there may be…

Home taping, especially given the facilities available to do it, has stripped a lot of the companies (recording, distributing, publishing, retailing) of large slices of their revenue. Wherever you care to look at the infrastructure as a whole, this is an irrefutable fact. I can justify home taping in many ways. I'm not actually in love with it because being an artist who by the nature of his material naturally attracts the less wealthy, I tend to be bootlegged more than most.

Even though I realise that it is taking from me, I couldn't react too harshly to the odd private tape. In terms of giving someone a souvenir of their night with you, you win a friend. You just hope that he can also give the authorised studio versions a chance.

In many cases the bootleggers are turning the contraband out on far superior equipment than the records were made on in the first place. It would be laughable really, if it wasn't such a killer.

The Business is such that only particular types of people would be involved in it for love. For their life's work, regardless of money. When you're in business, you're usually in it for what money can do for you, and when you've got enough money, you go off and do it.

Unless you are a big name artist, you are on the end of a commercial chain, and you are the last to be paid: *ie* artists are at the most risk when it comes to bankruptcies or misdealings further up the chain.

If the retailer goes bust, *no one* is paid. If the distributor goes bust, *only* the retailer is paid. If the record company goes bust, *everyone* gets their money *except* the artist. A bust record company has little and (most often) no effect at all on the retailer, the distributor, or the publisher – who has already had his money from them *before* the records are pressed. They are all recipients of the elusive spondulics. The only effect it has is on the artist, who does *not* get paid. At all. I have personal experiences. The hair in between my toes is curly.

There have been many bankruptcies or very close shaves further up the chain this last few years. Specifics... OK, I released a record called 'Once' through the now defunct Awareness label in the UK. We had a 'bite' from Miles Copeland, Sting's old manager, for the US rights.

When we met him he seemed very nervous indeed. I couldn't really work it out at the time, because it would seem that a man in his position would hardly be in awe of me, or anything remotely similar. However, he was definitely uneasy. We gave him the US rights and the record was released on his label, IRS. We were in pretty constant touch and before long we learned that they had sold 7,500 copies; at least it was a start, I thought. Then we ascertained, from the American publisher, some three or four months later that the figure was up to 13,000.

We started to ask for royalties... and they started making excuses. This went on for two or three weeks. Then the bombshell... they told us that most of the records had been returned! They had covered their tracks and what was left was quickly swept under the carpet. My British publisher, (Andy Heath of Momentum,) was powerless to uncover the truth, and I didn't have any money to fight it.

That record is still available in the USA, it can still be ordered: we did. I still haven't had a penny from them.

I know that Rory Gallagher was treated in the same way by the same people at the same time; and there were others. I remember that 'Dread Zeppelin' were later paid off in studio time, which was a poor exchange for the money they had lost.

For my last record, 'Death or Glory', I didn't get a penny from anywhere at all, but that's a different story. Only the people are similar.

I have a young Canadian friend, an extraordinary musician, a top drawer player. He is a member of a band called The Tea Party. They are very talented. Their record has just gone 'platinum' in Canada. They are $150,000 (Canadian) in debt. The only hope they have of getting out of debt is to go 'platinum' in the USA. Reason - *everyone* involved with them has been paid except them. Eg, two videos were made at a cost of $50,000 each.

I did the same thing. Had to. On paper I still owe EMI a spurious £70,000. I know that they've now written me off − killed in action. (By the time I actually depart the planet I'll probably have paid off another couple of grand.)

So, the artist is the most vulnerable. This does not really include the top two or three hundred whose names populate what I call the 'permanent chart'. (That's a particular kind of gravy train, on which the passengers talk in terms of Lear jets, and whether house number four is a luxury... or whatever.) I'm talking about artists who have maintained themselves despite the vagaries of fickle taste and with a consistent quality of achievement, and without a headline anywhere, for years.

Suffice to say that many people who populate the business are a little on the shady side. It can be very attractive in a man.

The Charts have been reasonably accessible to all comers during two brief periods of my career. The late sixties confusion and the mid seventies glut. I did make it once or twice after that, but they were flukes. All too often, the charts are manipulated by money and local retailers.

Some time ago, a friend of mine, who is one of the finest creative guitarists I've ever listened to, comforted me somewhat after I'd completely mislaid a wife (whilst we were talking about a youngish well-known 'classical' violin-player, who had been the subject of a massively successful marketing campaign) with: 'Well, they had the vocalists through, you know, Pavarotti and Domingo and the rest... what they needed after that was an instrumentalist or two, and he fitted the bill. He's just a marketing exercise. They proved that they could still do it; but he hasn't yet.'

And they can, and they will do so for as long as lining a nest is desirable, for as long as taking liberties with other people's lives is a decent sport. There'll be all the usual combinations, from the massive hype marketing operations, right the way down to back-street bootleg rip-off. From crazy discrimination to ignorant and clumsy corporate machinations.

During the 'Death or Glory' campaign we discovered that although we had sold enough copies to enter the 'Indie' charts, we didn't qualify, because we weren't being distributed by an 'independent' distributor – some of whom are virtual corporations, anyway. And ours was a one man record company!

It didn't unduly bother me because that was the kind of anachronistic sledgehammer that I had long since learned to come to terms with, but it sure did bother the record company. It was most definitely one of the shots that holed him. Mine was a technical knock-out, his was for real, and forever.

Would The Beatles have still been The Beatles had Brian Epstein not been able to fill an aircraft hanger with singles (and publicity) at the time?

I personally think that that wouldn't have made any difference, but what about all the other scams? Neil Christian and the Crusaders!!! Now there was a number… and wouldn't I have done it if I could? I couldn't. Which doesn't make me any better does it? I'm prone to a good scam.

It's usually good fun, but when that kind of behaviour is perpetrated too many times at the expense of too many others, then in my own mind, it would tend to become 'meglo'. Diseased. Cynical. Misanthropic. It's all a scam. The whole damned thing is a scam. The best you can hope for is a sketch!

Technology has improved to such a degree that it has not only brought the price down for serious recording in the bedroom, which is where many a hit is now made, but has miniaturised equipment to such a degree that the perceived difference between a record made at the Abbey Road studios and one made in a cubicle at Leicester Square gents is likely to be just a few extraneous sounds.

Anyone, but anyone, can now make a record, which has automatically taken a lot of the mystique out of getting together with a group of peers, getting some songs rehearsed, and being thrown into the 'studio' environment for a limited period, at the end of which the axe falls and you have to take what you've got: real life.

Ninety-nine per cent of the population under the age of forty now have, in their own homes, the ability to record sound or video, or both. I think I'll make a track on the telephone answering machine just for the hell of it.

However, technology has also handed the muse's traditional hunting grounds, the young hearts, to the machine, on a plate. The young have instant audio/visual access wherever they are, whether it be TV ads, computer game chip or supermarket propaganda sludge. What more do the great Nintendo masses need? When it comes to the end of the day for the Super Mario Twins, Debussy is a bit flat, and Chester Burnett doesn't come with rap visuals. Jesus! What have I just said?

Then there is the perceived technological future. This is carried around by people like Alan Sugar, the boffins at Sony, Stephen Hawking, Telecom, McLaren, Clive Sinclair etc., and a few adults. An immediate future looms in which buying a CD player is a real commitment. Because nothing is really standardised. Or ever will be until the ultimate format is a series 'Y' 8.9 Turbo and counting...

Rumours and counter rumours are bandied about, making the average buyer slightly wary of when the next major change in format is going to be sprung. You can take money that it will be at the beginning of the next perceived economic 'boom' period. But then there'll always be the failures.

Remember those great lumpy four-track cassettes for the car? I'm pleased to say that I never bought one. More recently there have been the various attempts at digital/laser video disc/tape types. Sure, I've got a few million smackers doing nothing... sure, okay... we'll have two in every bathroom.

Obsolescence has become dependable, and necessarily so. Music is not really the item being sold any more. What is really being sold is the ever improving apparatus (as mod furniture) for reproducing 'sounds' of some kind in ever more pristine condition. The kind of wallpaper players that William Morris might have been appalled to know that he'd canvassed the approach toward.

And they'll bootleg anything. They're intended to. Their manufacture is directed towards doing exactly that. You can only get a tenner for a record, but you can get back between twenty to a hundred times that for the machine to play and copy it on. Next to that, the music is worth very little.

One person can press 100,000 CDs, but it employs an army to manufacture the same amount of playing machines. (That'll change too). Low cost sperm, high cost egg. (That's changing even now!)

Wherever there is telephone or cable there already exists the means to pump your choice+ down the line at whatever hour you need it and for however long you want it. It will not be long before this arrives, along with the capability to inter-react with it.

Goodbye, record shops. Well, not quite, they'll just switch; there'll still be a big future in gardening tools as the boom generation move firmly into their slippers. Someone aged about twenty-eight right now is going to make an absolute killing amassing a chain of 'funeral homes', ready in time for the baby-boomers to pop their clogs. *Circa* 2020-2030 AD.

Murdoch and Branson will already have their fingers in the optical high fibre pie. Who needs a stereo system when they can fight Arnie, and win, in virtual reality, to a Casio rendition of 'Die Walküre' down at the re-vamped Virgin Mega-Reality?

The developing nations are sometimes a bane, and very often a blessing. I Have found myself bootlegged all over the world in poorer countries. In Portugal I once found the gig I had just played on sale in the street about an hour later. No point in even thinking about it.

I once discovered myself in a shop in Bahrain under Led Zeppelin. The recording had been made by 'LED ZEPPELIN AND ROY HARPER!', and you could hear the needle going down on the record it was copied from! No point in knowing about it.

The first pirate CD pressing plant in Venezuela will shortly be exporting its wares to Germany for a Deutschmark each. It'll be half-way kosher. It will take a little while before the holes are plugged. These CDs will arrive in the UK at a Dollar each! Goodbye Asda. (Artist at this point has long since gone – as is the journalist with the attitude. In twenty years time he'll be stuck in Woodstock with a bus pass, writing to the letters page of the *Banbury Mercury* on the incredible size of Lord Major's moustache, and on how less than wonderful it was to have had the recently deceased Salman Rushdie walking the streets again.)

In my own estimation, the under-developed nations are about to develop (round about right now), to such an extent that we are going to have to have a complete overhaul of our own perceptions of the way in which we approach growth, and work, in order to stay at anything like parity. Unless the CIA/Mafia wants to alter the progress, then China and India are two huge awakening economies, with kinetic blue touch paper in place. And they're neighbours. Money has been known to speak. Jabber jabber. TBC…

In my view, English is now established as the international language of the song. There are great songs in every language. There are great performers everywhere. It must sometimes be with much chagrin that the Francophiles peer across the twenty one miles at Dover only to see that the language of their ancient and annoying little adversary has assumed an international importance far in excess of what could now be attained by their own.

In true xenophobic tradition many media doors in France are now closed to non-Gallic thought. But who can blame the upkeep of a knee-jerk reaction to such leading existentialists as Cliff and Mary Whitehouse, not to mention Rolf and Mark Almond? They'd maybe have done better to have embraced the lot, because what they've effectively said to the rest of the world is 'No more singing nuns for you lot then', and proceeded to shoot their own international aspirants in the fanny, severing them from any hope of hybrid health.

Even though English via America must be distastefully insidious to a French person who sees that valuable elements of his/her culture are in danger of extinction, language could never have prohibited Edith Piaf from the galactic audience she will always deserve. Ah, well, there's always Daniel Lanois, and Quebec, and the McGarrigle sisters.

The language that is spoken by the most people is Mandarin Chinese. I don't see this changing until the Mafia drop the bomb. The other languages spoken by the most people are Russian, Spanish, and of course English. The point with English is that anyone can speak it badly and be understood. You can't do that in German, and whenever I have tried doing it in French in France I just get looked straight through, like I don't exist. Maybe I don't?

The point here is that as the world languages – and by implication, cultures – begin to amalgamate, English will have a huge put into the pot. Whether there are winners and/or losers anymore is open to conjecture... and your own interpretation of the particular sport you wish to engage in, and whether you think that nationalism really does mean anything that profound to anyone with any intelligence, any more …in the final analysis, to anyone at all …or certainly to anyone else.

'Home' can mean tender thoughts, but the rest is surely jingo in this developing world. You may not be able to love your neighbour but surely you can appreciate him.

Do you really win by subjugating everyone else to your own culture, or have you lost most of the transmittable, tangible, touchable everyday elements of your own by so-doing anyway? By venturing a car park too far into the abstraction of the 'global'?

By the attempt to become all things to all women… Whatever…? Tears to feed the seed to grow the new genetically engineered crop.

The possible artistic results here are that permutations between 'Imagine' and 'Guantanamera'…(the writer of which was never paid a dime) and some choice Kimeo Eto will keep creative music alive well into the era of the Martian arrival. Keep on rockin' in the Mardi Gras will run… and some.

Pidgin English and pidgin Spanish will do well together, with the odd Chinese or Japanese word or parable thrown in. It'll be all-in. There'll be bits of Russian bleak, Italian style and French cuisine.

The economic implications of the coming of the world are interesting. The developing countries will suddenly gain long overdue power. The power to be able to put African and South American rhythms together outside of Cuba. Whole new species are likely.

The accessibility of your own choice of music in your own home will hit the developing world as it did us in the '50s. As south east Asia and south America get the cash, there'll be music revolutions. Unless Decca can mount an all-out counter campaign immediately. With Montgomery at the helm.

Get the girls in India together with the boys in Brazil. It's not predictable, you are not going to be able to tell what is going to blend and why. You can have a few guesses, they may be near but they won't be right. We are now tasting the magic of the future. In our own case it was built by Johann Strauss, Fred Nietzche, WC Handy, Leadbelly, Keats, Davis, Guthrie, Gershwin, Shakespeare *et al*. This list will be expanded by the grandchildren of kids now living in poverty along the Yangtze.

The economics of the near future will bring people together who knew nothing of each other's culture fifty years previously. They will be brought together by the greatest upheaval in human history. By looking into the great media mirror. There they will see themselves. They will see war, famine, boom, disease, beauty, greed... the full monte, and be increasingly aware of it in increasing numbers.

Money will change hands, deals will be done. The business structures we now see in embryonic forms will be developed more surely over the next few decades. One of those forces, the black market, is huge, an unstoppable major force. A natural check on runaway authority, whether such authority be hard-nosed or benign.

Bootlegging of everything will be endemic. It may not be as profitable with music as we now know it, because a lot of music is likely to become the equivalent of a packet of crisps, and will be accessible at every point and because of technology, could become virtually free. PRS will seem like The South Sea Bubble.

Many more people will be able to achieve higher musical proficiency status, (and not earn as much for it!). There are genius' in the jungles of Tasmania. Perlman will be surpassed in technique, and artistry. Shakespeare will be much harder to catch, but someone who has the untold stories and fables of a thousand years at his disposal will make the attempt. The Uruguay round has already initiated that.

In short, the sooner the human world comes to terms with genuine equanimity, then the sooner the big share-out happens and war, greed and megalomania cease to be the governing factors they still are today. How very primitive it all is four hundred and forty seven years after the death of the megalomaniac Henry VIII. To the day! (Jan 28th).

It was Henry of course who first uttered the unutterable, that God was a bit of an iffy proposition, at least in the hands of anyone other than himself. In all probability it was this rather simple proposition that freed Billy up about a generation later to go off and write everything that had been thought and spoken but no one had ever dared commit to paper because of perceptions of blasphemy, fears of being burned alive and various other ways of getting yourself completely snookered.

Once the big blasphemy had occurred however, and had actually been perpetrated by the King himself, it became open season. Pistol was allowed to be a spineless half-wit rogue, in public. Falstaff was allowed to be seen cursing, and rotting to death on drink. It must have been hilarious at The Globe... 'All the world's a stage...' became true. Condoned public ribaldry. Romeo climbing the ivy for a necking session, Lear in memory, dotage and confusion. The frightening Macbeth and the tear-jerking Isolde.

Then Richard The Third, the most convincing piece of Tudor propaganda ever written. And all in all, generally, good honest profanity unleashed at last! ...TBC, maybe.

But how does the artist on the bread-line continue to exist, continue to be able to afford not getting involved with the Social Security? One, marry someone rich and beautiful in body and mind ...okay... Two, win the lottery. Three, do everything yourself. Three wins. A walkover. All that remains to be done is to trot down the Rowley Mile and collect the wherewithal.

How is 'three' to be achieved? By never letting any detail out of your sight, ever again. By claiming, cadging, cajoling and grabbing everything that you ever made, and giving it back to the person that it really belongs to, namely yourself. (The music 'industry', in many cases, has had it for the best part of thirty years, and has not even bothered to try to sell it most of the time, never mind understand any of it.)

By then building up a list of actual real people who would be interested in having copies of your work, and finally, by selling it to them cheaper than any retailer could do, by post. My first such project was the re-release of 'Flat, Baroque and Berserk' (with 'I Hate the White Man' and 'Another Day' etc.)

It is a limited edition, signed, and comes in a presentation box. Included are a forty page book on the making of the record, those involved, and my thoughts on it, with various contributions, and a colour Festival Hall poster of the time. The cost is twenty pounds. It would be at least thirty in any shop. And the rest. There are about three thousand left.

*Commercial break:* for more details, write to...

3 Norton Park Crescent, Sheffield S8 5GN

The intention is to use the cash to manufacture all of my favourites in this way. The next four to be done will be 'Stormcock', 'HQ', 'Bullinamingvase', and 'The Unknown Soldier' – the last three have yet to be released on CD. I don't think that there will be any more limited editions, the signing of them all alone would be unrepeatable. They'll just be up to scratch, integral, finally.

All my records will be redone with the care that they deserve. We intend to bring the prices as far down as we can, and once we are into the third and fourth CD, with less overheads, I shouldn't see why we couldn't at the very least half that price for some of the records. The three that I'm not that keen on, 'Burn the World', 'Come Out Fighting Ghengis Smith' and 'Work of Heart' are likely to be buried somewhere in Finchley pet cemetery.

The first initial re-releases of the whole catalogue are now up and running. Because they were made in Austria, which has been some distance away for a while now, there are still some errors in the pictorial and literary matter surrounding them.

Like for instance, the 'new' 'temporary' cover of the last record, 'Death or Glory', isn't yet up to standard, and so there will only be very few of these available before a less hasty, more appropriate job can be done, which will obviously include the correction of all the mistakes in the original lyric book as well!, etc, etc...

This is what I have wanted to do for some years now. To get everything I ever made back into the spirit of the way in which it was originally conceived. They are nearly all huge canvases comprising copious amounts of elements which are at this moment lying around disintegrating. At last I'm free and I'm getting started. Works straight from the artist to the listener. A little piece of me, straight to you. Something that I have made myself, and had hold of myself, and signed for you, in your hands. No more impersonal crap. Touch.

Music no longer comes to you, you have to seek it out, and sometimes you will really have to look very hard indeed. As always it'll be worth it. Those who have done this all their lives because music is part of their *raison d'être* will not have too many problems. What we will be missing is the mass 'appreciation' that we had in the '70s. We'll have to move to India or Brazil for that, but that'll be in about a decade or so.

The beauty and the horror is that 'The new street rhythms of Rio' will be available to us all on floppy within the next month or two.

That's not to say that you can't be turned on by the theme music to the Ariston ad, and consequently get into deepest Laurie Anderson. It's just that the 'buzz' has gone, been forced out, temporarily, from one of the great primeval forces of life... music. But only in the west. It would have happened naturally anyway.

The economies, bootlegging, the impending share-out and general corruption all have their little parts to play in the demise. We could have prolonged the life of the British music business by a decade or two at least, if we'd have stuck together and appreciated each other for our separate talents, but we couldn't.

There has been some amusement for me in relating our behaviour to that which typified us at the beginning of the Roman invasion. Instead of banding together and solidifying gains, we all waited in line for our own turn to fight, and then we fought against ourselves. Old habits...

Mock battles raged between posturing non-entities in posturing non-entities like the *New Musical Express* and the even newer *Q* magazine. We allowed apathy, stupidly myopic programming, vengeful journalism, silly cliques, intentional misunderstandings, disorganisation, jealousies, lies and general back-biting to undermine most of the original altruistic intention.

To all intents and purposes, music died in us for long periods of time. The consequence to the industry is catastrophic. Without the continuous promotion of new and timeless talent in its own timeless atmospheres, inspired by respected antecedents, (and encouraged by a healthy press), it died to the same extent. The re-investment was non-existent. A load of young talent with no industry left. A lot of accomplished young players on the dole.

No worries, as Rolf would say, it'll spring up somewhere else, and the present helmsmen will all be foreigners. Their descendants might have luck on their side to some degree though, because it's probable that English will still be involved. Somewhere?! Maybe!? And the structures will survive a little longer, perhaps... Oh dear, what the hell am I talking about?

Until the latest universal exigency requires the new ultimate universal formatting job, the brain implant, at which point I would have been glad that I wasn't around any longer, ...if I'd been around. Ever. At all. Thorny problem that one. 'Ne'er moind', as they'd say down on the Marlborough Ups, 'The next ice-age'll take care of that'. Along with Barclaycard, Bourton-On-The-Water and that silly statue of the pantomime George the Third on his way out of some even sillier business in Trafalgar Square, London W1.

I love music. It has inspired me and allowed me to understand much about the world I know. Every song I have written has moved me at some point. How empty it would have been to have written songs, or postcards, that hadn't.

****

Just in case anyone wondered, I think that I've had a terrific life, a charmed existence, and I wouldn't have swapped it for anything. I've had a great time here. My love to you.

Meanwhile, The Flood, The Earthquake, The Next Ice-age, and other Acts of the Great Denture, more movements of the Great Stool.

'I don't know whether he's in flagrant revolt against accepted standards of civilised behaviour or if he's just being deeply conformist to his peer group!'

# 23

# John Otway

## ...on becoming a failure.

This is the story of how I became a great failure. It's the story about writing a book and being discovered by a bright publisher who could spot a star in freefall and give him a helping shove in the downward direction. It's also about landing quite softly and finding oneself not in the jaws of an abyss, but oddly in a rather pleasant enjoyable fertile valley.

Admittedly the genesis of the whole thing did begin at a rather bleak period. I had managed to cock-up all the aspects of my life simultaneously. With another couple, I bought a house to convert into two flats. Three quarters of the way through the work, when my friends flat was completed and I had a building site with no roof, work was halted by the council. The lease specifically forbade any such conversion.

I had also just fired my agent, believing I could do the work better myself, only to discover that my live audience – my only regular source of income – could be reduced to three people a night, given incorrect handling. Finally, my Canadian wife packed her bags. She decided, probably very accurately, that the grass was greener almost anywhere else.

The idea of a book was suggested by a writer friend who told me that there was a shortage of books about music. As I'd had an interesting career, it was quite possible that my autobiography would find a publisher. I thought about the idea, and by the time I had written the first couple of pages life had started to look quite a lot rosier. I had found a new girl-friend and was in that period of romance when even a flat-less, gig-less, hit-less life looks sweet.

I did not find it difficult to write. Being an egocentric show off, 70,000 words about myself was actually a pleasant distraction from my other problems. As I intended to make money out of this venture, I felt I was doing something positive about my problems by writing about myself. No discipline was involved. I was writing constantly: at home on my word processor, on the tube, on my way to a gig, backstage. The story of my life was a particularly easy birth.

I made two decisions. One, that I would concentrate on the cock-ups and disasters of my career; and two, that I would write in the third person. The first few paragraphs of 'Cor Baby That's Really Me' give a good idea of the style:

*'The summer of '78, John Otway stood on a stage built in the Market Square of his home town Aylesbury. The police had sealed off the town centre, ATV were filming the event for his own 40 minute TV show to be screened on national television, and 10,000 locals turned up to witness the event.*

*The TV programme was to be called* Stardustman *- about a local dustman who always believed he was a star and went on to make a hit record. The producers of the show hopefully felt that Otway was going to make more than one hit record, and they would have a valuable piece of vintage footage. In the same way, his record company also hoped he would have lots more hits and gave him a quarter of a million in the way of encouragement. Both, along with Otway himself, were to be sadly disappointed.*

*This is the story of that dustman, who fought tooth and nail to become a star, only to have to fight tooth and nail not to become a dustman again. Parts of it you may find amusing, parts sad, occasionally enlightening but quite often you may just think "What a prat." There was a very similar feeling among a large group of pupils at the Grange County Secondary School in Aylesbury one winter lunchtime. Our fourteen-year-old hero had gathered together an audience of 100 to witness him down a complete bottle of ink in one. They stood there speechless as he poured the blue liquid down his throat, and then complained bitterly that he had been given Stevenson's instead of Quink.*

*A few of the audience found this event amusing, a few sad, the occasional person there who was strangely attracted to this rather odd youth found it enlightening, but quite a lot did think, "What a prat." Their opinion did not change a great deal when Otway complained for days afterwards that his pee had turned blue.'*

Most people who read the manuscript found it amusing. However, getting a publisher took over a year. I found sending unsolicited manuscripts to publishers just as constructive as sending demo tapes to record companies. Many companies, I am sure, reckoned that if I could not sell records and could only get three people a night to see the live show, I was not going to sell very many books.

They all read the manuscript though, and were quite encouraging in their rejections suggesting many rival publishers whom they felt needed this kind of book.

In the end I considered self-publishing, in my case the direct opposite to vanity publishing. A friend approached the manager of a local book shop who passed my writings on to a distributor whose best mate happened to commission books for Omnibus Press. It was like discovering that the manager of your local record store was the key to your recording deal with CBS.

I met Frank Warren in a pub in the heart of Soho for a couple of pints at the end of the working day. He had read my book, was very amused, but did not know how to sell it. Omnibus largely did biographies of people like Kylie Minogue, Take That and other equally famous people of the day. Taking on John Otway was a departure from the company's normal policy.

'We usually deal with successful popular subjects,' he said, 'but this book is not about that is it?' We both agreed it was unlike any other they had on their catalogue. Several pints later we found the solution to that particular hurdle by not trying to sell me as a success at all. Two pints later the whole marketing strategy was devised.

It was the cover that shocked me. I was obviously aware that the whole tome was full of self effacing humour, but that cover had 'Rock and Roll's Greatest Failure' above the title and stars and flashes announcing 'Bad Records' and 'Rank Incompetence' under the author's name. There was no let up on the back either, 'A tale of blind ambition and rank incompetence, and a salutary lesson for the aspiring musician on how not to achieve greatness.' it read.

I realised that in order to promote my book I needed to become Rock and Roll's Greatest Failure incarnate. But there was the obvious paradox in that if I was this failure I would not even have achieved one hit, and would certainly not be able to get a respectable publisher to publish my memoirs.

There is, or at least was in the case of this book, a long lead-up time between signing the contract and the release date, five months, enough time to acclimatise myself to my new role.

I was aided in my claim of great failure by the fact that I'd ended the book at the disastrous part of my life I described earlier. Since then Karen my girlfriend had become pregnant, I had moved into her lovely garden flat in Southfields, and the birth of my daughter Amy Otway added considerably to our general happiness. I'd sold out my share of my old semi-converted flat, live work was largely back on its feet and I'd also got a small but lucrative acting role in a new TV series 'Forever Green'.

The publisher and I arranged a pretty good promotional package. As well as the book, I would release a CD which could be the soundtrack. It would feature all the tracks that had been so unhelpful to my career - a sort of aid to help the reader understand exactly why things had taken the direction they had. I was able to book some thirty two dates in May following the London Book launch gig, and Omnibus were very pleased. I believe I was the first author they had that had done a 'book tour' alongside the signings.

For me it was like entering a strange world. People who deal with books are largely more serious and learned than those that inhabit the world of punk rock, and although I offered to sing a few songs in the shops I was visiting, nearly all preferred me to sit quietly at a desk with a glass of water and just sign books for the unusual bunch of customers that had arrived to buy them.

The first signing I did was in my home town of Aylesbury. The last author that had been to this shop for this purpose was Bill Oddie promoting a book about birds. I was told not to expect too much as he had only sold two books in the hour that he was there. From that point onwards I referred to a quantity of two books as 'An Oddie'. As my book dealt for a large part with my childhood in the town, and as I had written about local characters, I did surprisingly well and signed a total of fifteen Oddies. The book signings were fun and I'm glad to say that the smallest number we ever did was in Edinburgh, during the cup final. One and a half Oddies.

The tour went well and gathered momentum as a larger number than normal turned out to see Rock and Roll's greatest failure on the road.

The most fun of all though was the interviews. For the whole of my career I had been doing interviews with the sole purpose of persuading people that my latest record was the best thing I'd ever done, and that it was about to give me back the sort of stardom I so obviously deserved. Because of the gap between recording and releasing these records and having seen the initial reaction, it was usually obvious to both myself and the interviewer that this was not going to happen. Also there is not a great deal to say about a record. The questions and answers are largely both routine and tedious.

Interviewer: 'So you've got a new single out. Tell me about it.'

Otway: 'Well I wrote the song about six months ago and played it to the band and they thought it would make a good single, so we went into the studio and recorded it. Now we're on tour to promote it and it seems to be going very well. We're really happy with the results and are hoping for a hit.'

Interviewer: 'Well, I wish you the best of luck with it.'

Interviewers are generally kind to struggling artists, and in my time I've done my fair share of the struggling.

But this was different; this was fun.

Interviewer: 'Why do you think you have been so unsuccessful?'

Otway: 'Well, for a number of reasons. Firstly a lack of talent hasn't really helped much. And when I was lucky, like when I had my hit, I seemed to be one of those people who could always turn any promising situation to my disadvantage.'

Interviewer: 'You're not seriously saying that you haven't any talent, are you?'

Otway: 'Well we can put it to the test, here's my CD there are twenty one tracks on it. One of those tracks is a hit, the rest are flops. Let's pick one of those flops at random, play it and then decide.

I was in my element. The humour of my show had always relied on my ability to laugh at myself and this vehicle was perfect for driving that humour home. I must have been good at it. I did more interviews around that time than I had done for years: Radio 1, Radio 4, lots of local TV and radio, *The Sunday Correspondent* and the *Independent*. Lots and lots.

Two of them stick out in my mind. Jonathan Ross had me on his chat show on the same day as the Brit Awards. I was supposed to be the exact opposite to the winners celebrating on the other channel. The other was *The Daily Mirror*, who did a whole page feature. It was my largest piece of national press, so far.

The *Mirror* interview took place in a pub at midday. After several pints at that early hour of the drinking day, I was holding court marvellously, going over the top about just what a disaster area I was. I had done many interviews by this time, and knew precisely where my weak points were, and where I was most vulnerable. I was like a fully developed negative. I convinced the Fleet Street hack that I was indeed the personification of all that is not worthy in the land of Rock 'n' Roll. Several days later the piece came out. 'WHAT A PRAT I AM!' screamed the headline, alongside a large colour photograph that managed to say just as much as the words.

I whooped with delight as I read the piece in my local newsagents before buying up every copy in the shop and rushing home to show everyone. Karen felt that this was going too far, so did a lot of other people. 'But you're not a prat,' they would insist, and I – by now having lived the character for a while – did not know whether to argue or agree. But I was pleased that Amy was still a baby, and was not at school with the other children saying "Ere is your Dad the Prat?'

The result of all this publicity was a book that sold very well, and a very happy publisher. Very quickly 'Cor Baby That's Really Me', the story of my life, was to outsell all the records I had released since the hit. The 'Soundtrack' CD was also doing pretty well, and it would appear that I had done something right.

Being a failure was a turning point for me, and the quality of life improved in its aftermath. Interestingly, I realised that beneath all the humour there was more than a little truth in the tag I had chosen. I was just very fortunate in that a lot of the disasters and ridiculous decisions I was responsible for were extreme enough to be funny. Ironically I ended up making money out of all the things I had cocked up so badly.

And the book. It's just sold its first print run and is going in to a second edition. How's that for failure?

# 24
# John Cooper Clarke

...misses the 'Rock Talk' dead-line by a mile, but graciously allows us to take a journey down memory lane, back to...

**beezley street**

far flung crazy pavements crack
the sound of empty rooms
a clinical arrangement
a dirty afternoon
where the fecal germs of mr freud
are rendered obsolete
the legal term is null and void
in the case of beezley street

in the cheap seats where murder breeds
somebody is out of breath
sleep is a luxury they don't need
a sneak preview of death
deadly nightshade is your flower
manslaughter your meat
spend a year in a couple of hours

on the edge of beezley street
where the action isn't
that's where it is
state your position
vacancies exist
in an x certificate exercise
ex servicemen explete
keith joseph smiles and a baby dies
in a box on beezley street

from the boarding houses and the bedsits
full of accidents and fleas
somebody gets it
where the missing persons freeze
wearing dead men's overcoats
you can't see their feet
a riff joint shuts and opens up
right down on beezley street

cars collide colours clash
disaster movie stuff
for the man with the fu manchu moustache
revenge is not enough
there's a dead canary on a swivel seat
there's a rainbow in the road
meanwhile on beezley street
silence is the mode

it's hot beneath the collar
it's cold beneath the balls
where the perishing stink of squalor
impregnates the walls
the rats have all got rickets
they spit through broken teeth
a blood stain is your ticket

one way down beezley street
the gangster and his hired hat
drive a borrowed car
he looks like the duke of edinburgh
but not so lah-di-dah
OAP mother-to be
watch that three-piece suite
when shitstopper drains
and crocodile skis
are seen on beezley street

in the kingdom of the blind
where the one eyed man is king
beauty problems are redefined
the doorbells do not ring
light bulbs pop like blisters
the only form of heat
where a fellow sells his sister
down the river on beezley street

the boys are on the wagon
the girls are on the shelf
their common problem
is that they're not someone else
the dirt blows out
the dust blows in
you can't keep it neat
it's a fully furnished dustbin
16 beezley street

vince the ageing savage
betrays no kind of life
but the smell of yesterday's cabbage
and the ghost of last year's wife
through a constant haze
of deodorant sprays
he says retreat
alsatians dog the dirty days

down the middle of beezley street
eyes dead as viscous fish
look around for laughs
if i could have just one wish
i would be a photograph
on this permanent monday morning
get lost or fall asleep
when the yellow cats are yawning
round the back of beezley street

people turn to poison quick
as lager turns to piss
sweethearts are physically sick
every time they kiss
it's a sociologist's paradise
each day repeats
uneasy cheesy greasy queasy beastly beezley street

_'They're looking for a music critic for the "Oldie"!'_